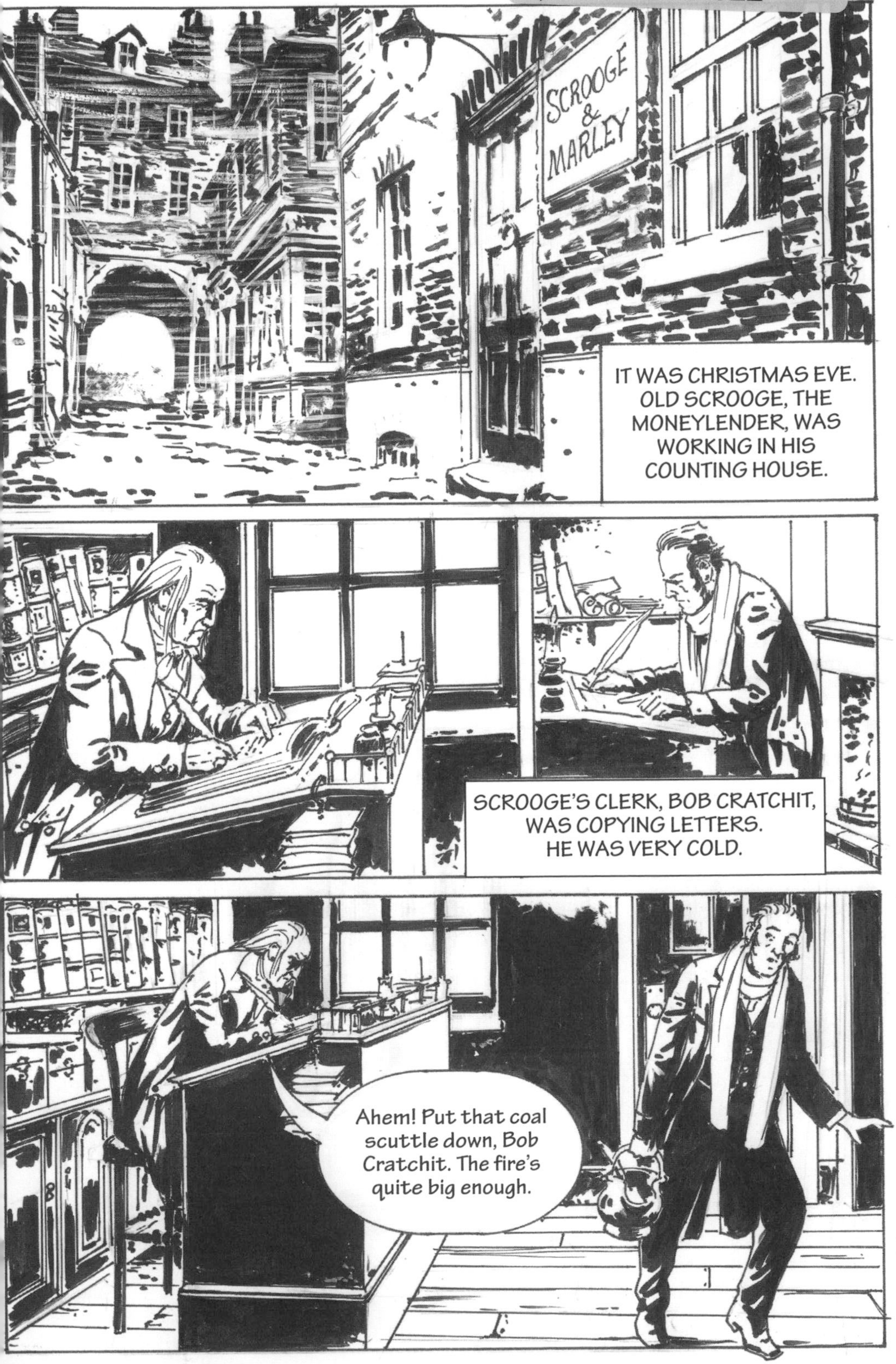
SCROOGE & MARLEY
IT WAS CHRISTMAS EVE. OLD SCROOGE, THE MONEYLENDER, WAS WORKING IN HIS COUNTING HOUSE.
SCROOGE'S CLERK, BOB CRATCHIT, WAS COPYING LETTERS. HE WAS VERY COLD.
Ahem! Put that coal scuttle down, Bob Cratchit. The fire's quite big enough.

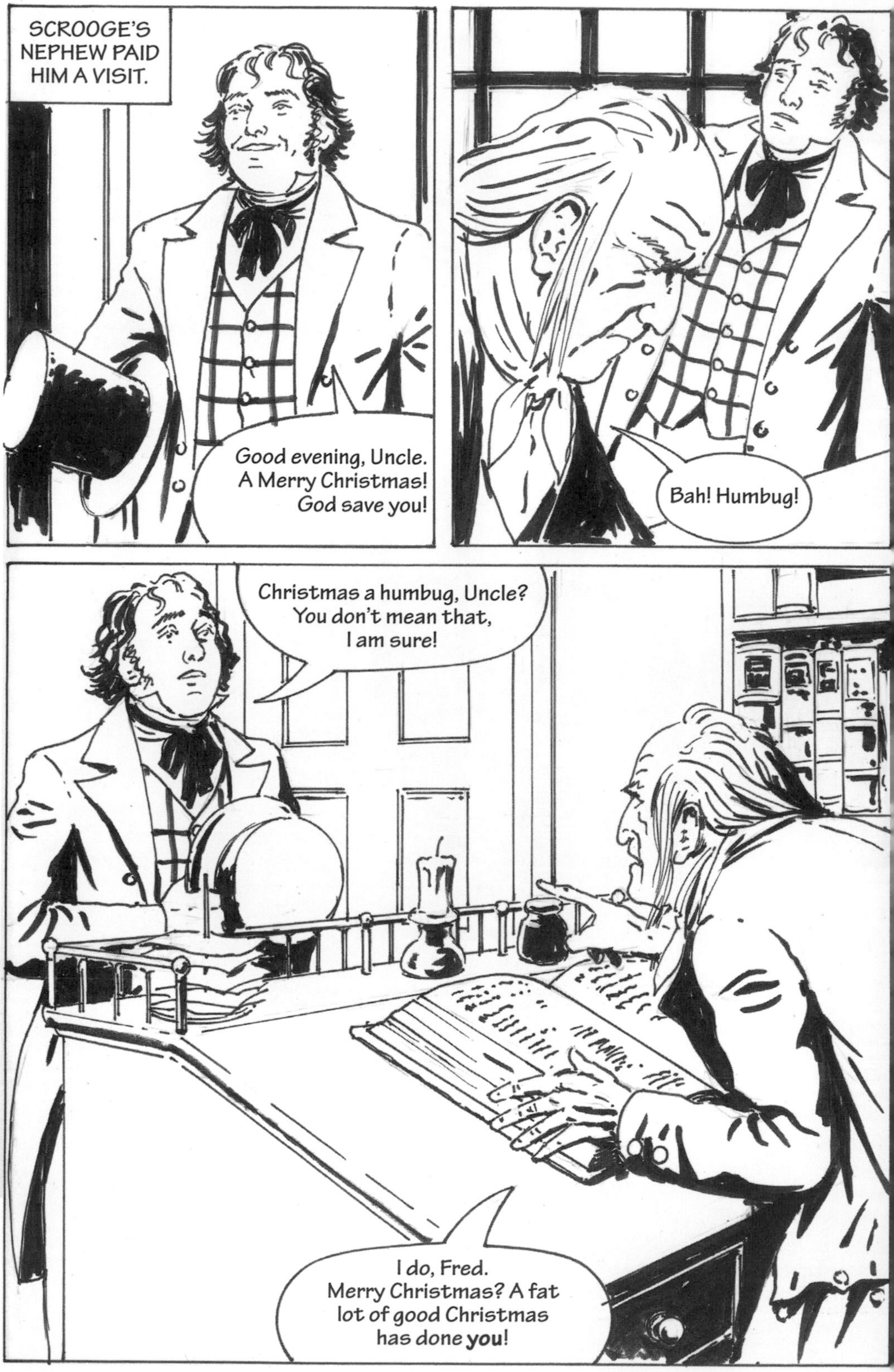
SCROOGE'S NEPHEW PAID HIM A VISIT.
Good evening, Uncle. A Merry Christmas! God save you!
Bah! Humbug!
Christmas a humbug, Uncle? You don't mean that, I am sure!
I do, Fred. Merry Christmas? A fat lot of good Christmas has done **you**!

Graphic Dickens

A CHRISTMAS CAROL

Retold by Hilary Burningham
Illustrated by Bob Moulder

WAKEFIELD LIBRARIES

30000010329581

ReadZone Books Limited

50 Godfrey Avenue
Twickenham
TW2 7PF
UK

WAKEFIELD LIBRARIES
& INFO. SERVICES

30000010329581	
Bertrams	20/11/2014
GRA	£7.99

For Celia

© in text Hilary Burningham 2014
© in illustrations Bob Moulder 2014
© in this edition ReadZone Books Limited 2014

Hilary Burningham has asserted her right under the Copyright Designs
and Patents Act 1988 to be identified as the author of this work.

Bob Moulder has asserted his right under the Copyright Designs
and Patents Act 1988 to be identified as the illustrator of this work.

British Library Cataloguing in Publication Data (CIP) is available
for this title.

Printed in Great Britain by Ashford Colour Press Ltd, Gosport

Every attempt has been made by the Publisher to secure appropriate
permissions for material reproduced in this book. If there has been any
oversight we will be happy to rectify the situation in future editions or
reprints. Written submissions should be made to the Publisher.

All rights reserved. No part of this publication may be reproduced,
stored in a retrieval system or transmitted, in any form or by any
means, electronic, mechanical, photocopying, recording or otherwise,
without the prior permission of ReadZone Books Limited.

ISBN 978 1 78322 013 7

Visit our website: www.readzonebooks.com

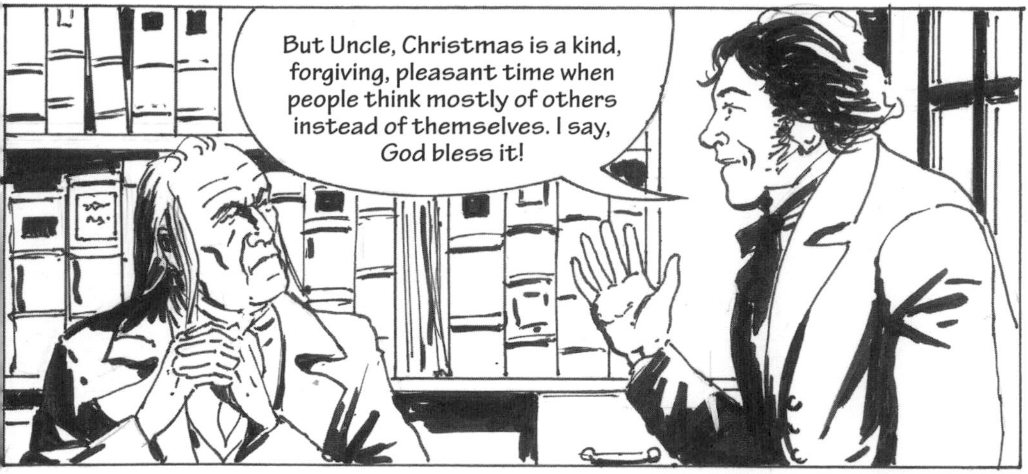
But Uncle, Christmas is a kind, forgiving, pleasant time when people think mostly of others instead of themselves. I say, God bless it!

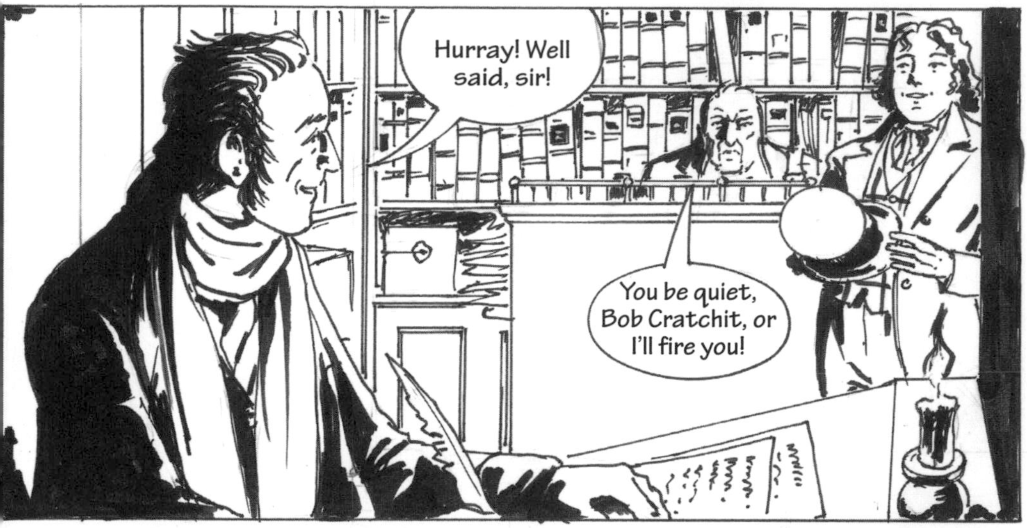
Hurray! Well said, sir!
You be quiet, Bob Cratchit, or I'll fire you!

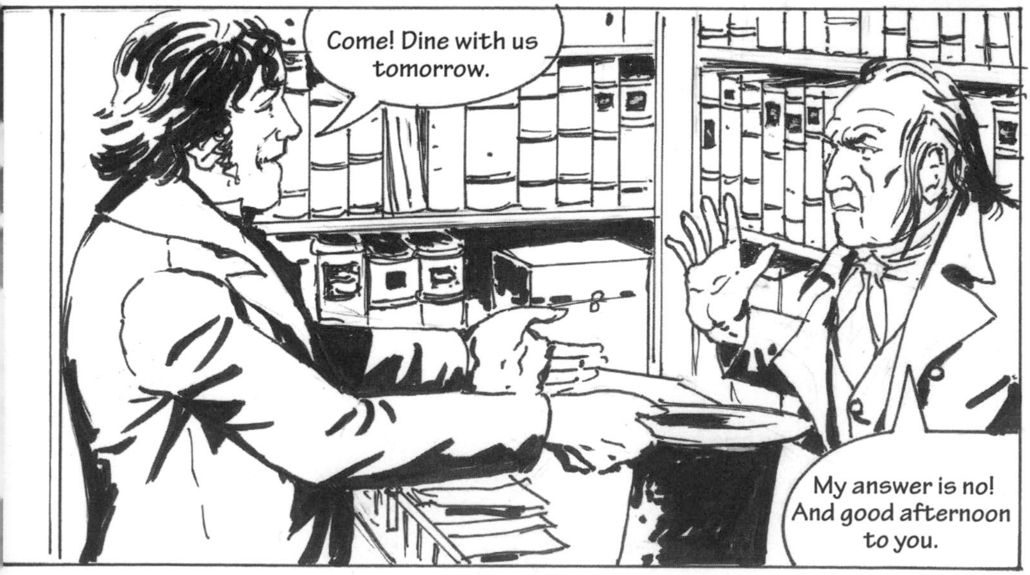
Come! Dine with us tomorrow.
My answer is no! And good afternoon to you.

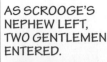

AS SCROOGE'S NEPHEW LEFT, TWO GENTLEMEN ENTERED.

Have I the pleasure of speaking to Mr Scrooge or Mr Marley?

Mr Marley died seven years ago this very night. Please state your business. I'm very busy.

At this joyful season of the year, Mr Scrooge, we are collecting money to help the poor.

Are there no prisons?

Plenty of prisons.

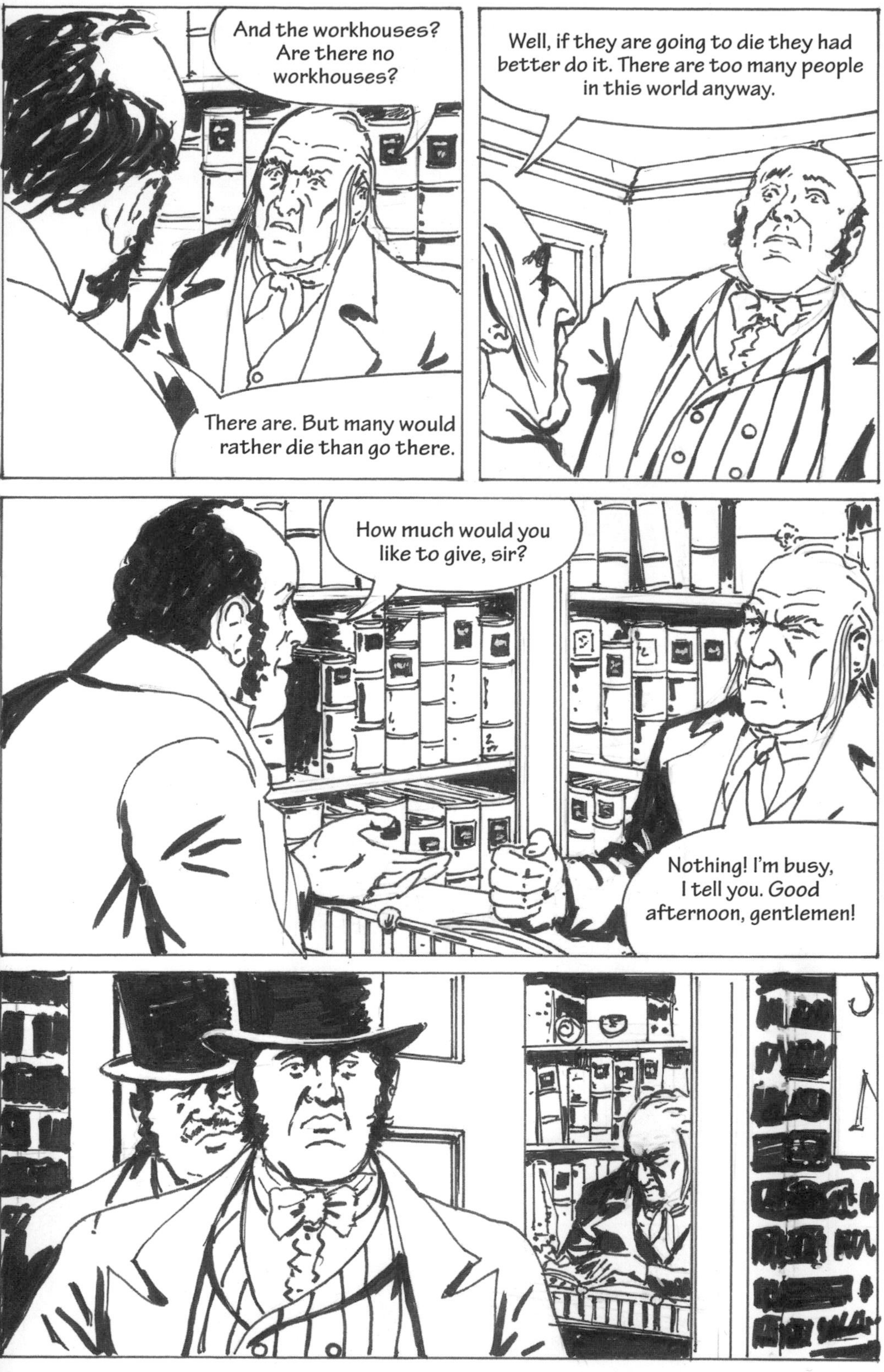

And the workhouses? Are there no workhouses?
There are. But many would rather die than go there.
Well, if they are going to die they had better do it. There are too many people in this world anyway.
How much would you like to give, sir?
Nothing! I'm busy, I tell you. Good afternoon, gentlemen!

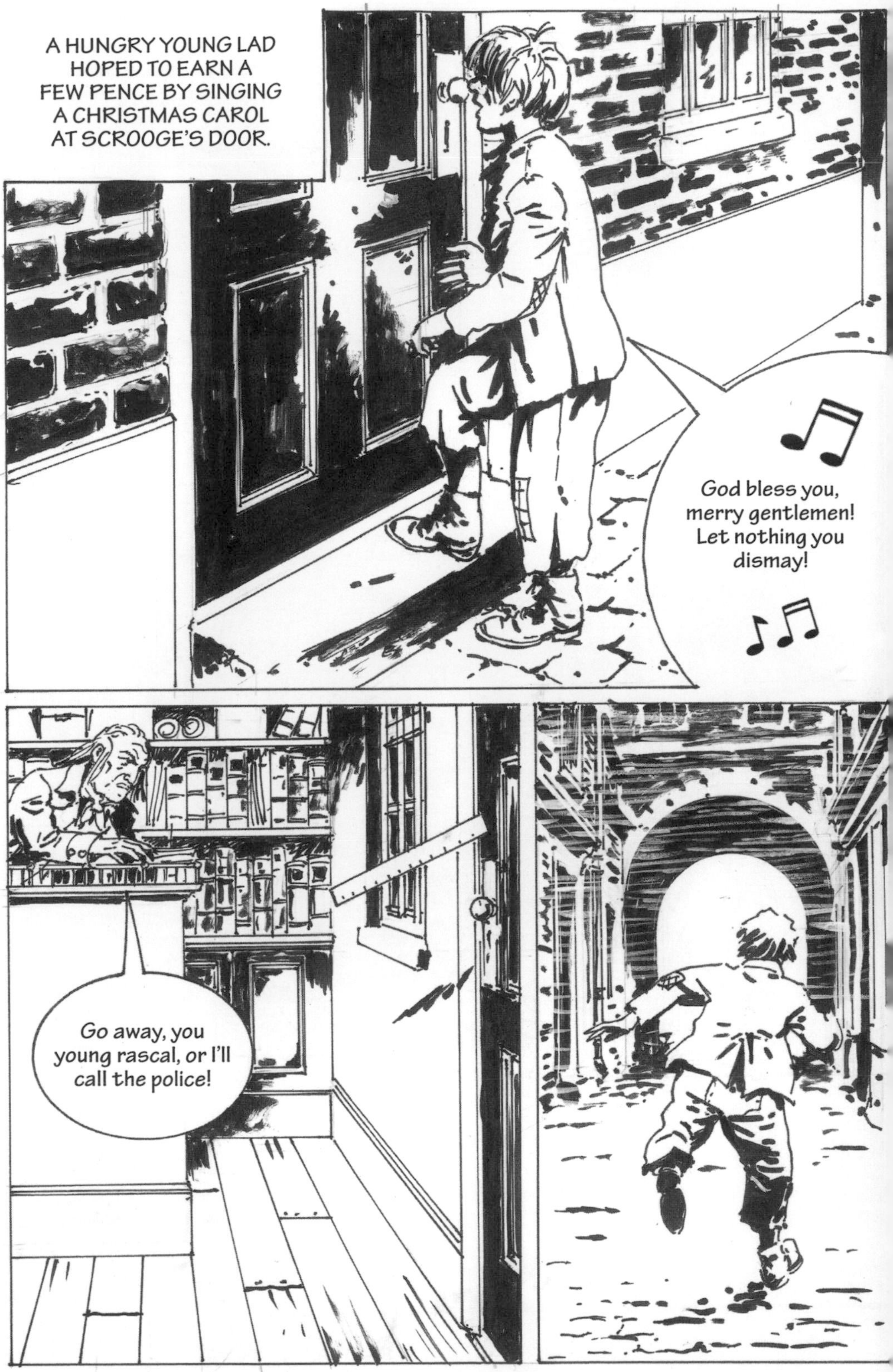
A HUNGRY YOUNG LAD HOPED TO EARN A FEW PENCE BY SINGING A CHRISTMAS CAROL AT SCROOGE'S DOOR.
God bless you, merry gentlemen! Let nothing you dismay!
Go away, you young rascal, or I'll call the police!

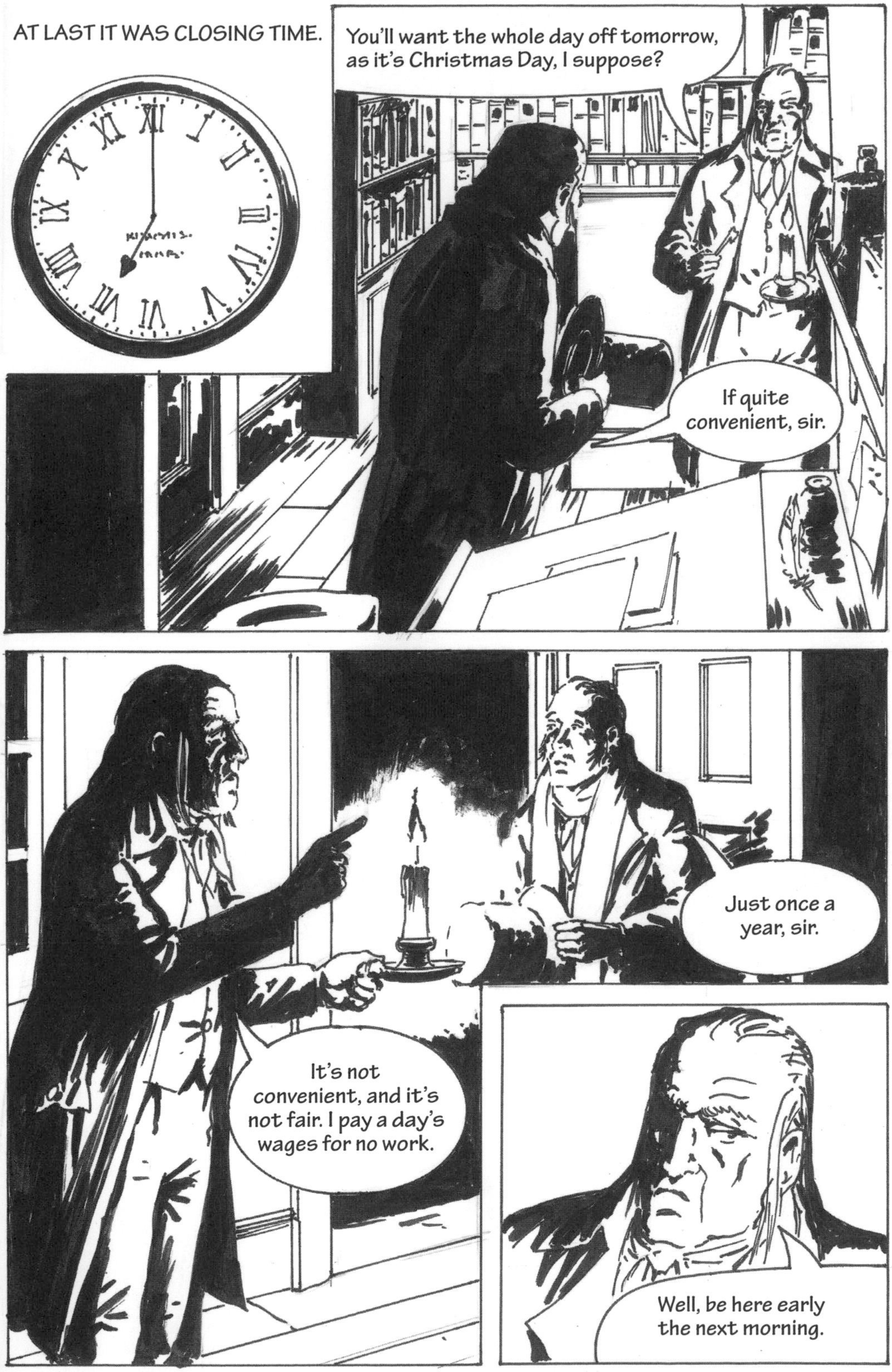
AT LAST IT WAS CLOSING TIME.
You'll want the whole day off tomorrow, as it's Christmas Day, I suppose?
If quite convenient, sir.
It's not convenient, and it's not fair. I pay a day's wages for no work.
Just once a year, sir.
Well, be here early the next morning.

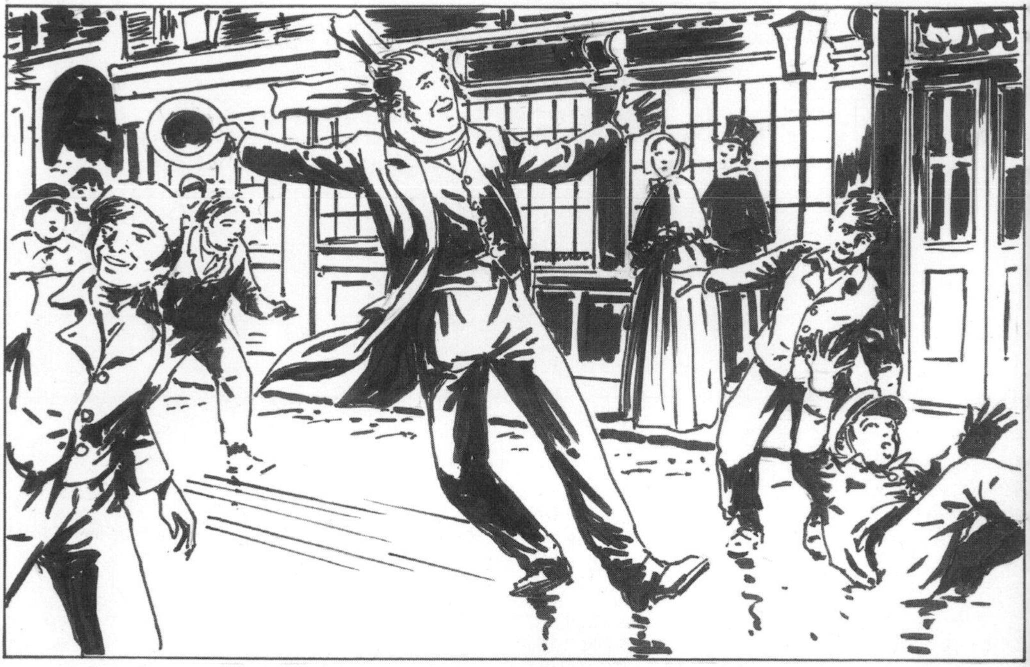

ON HIS WAY HOME, BOB JOINED SOME CHILDREN AT PLAY.

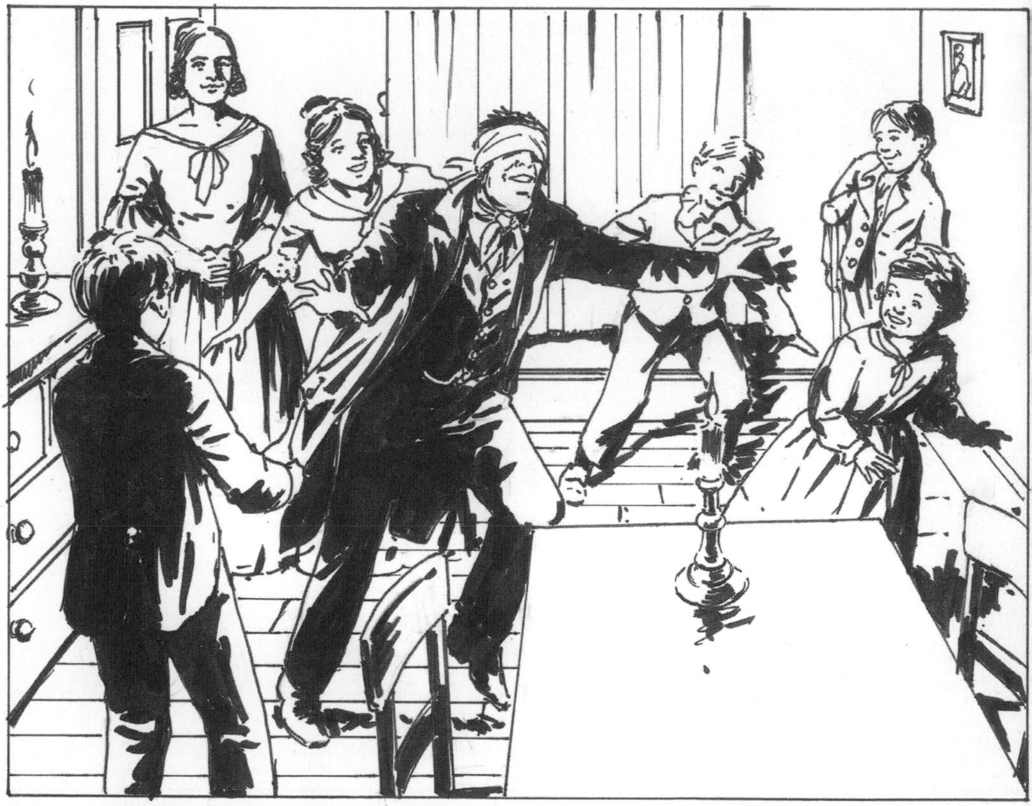

AT HOME, HE PLAYED A GAME OF BLIND MAN'S BUFF WITH HIS CHILDREN.

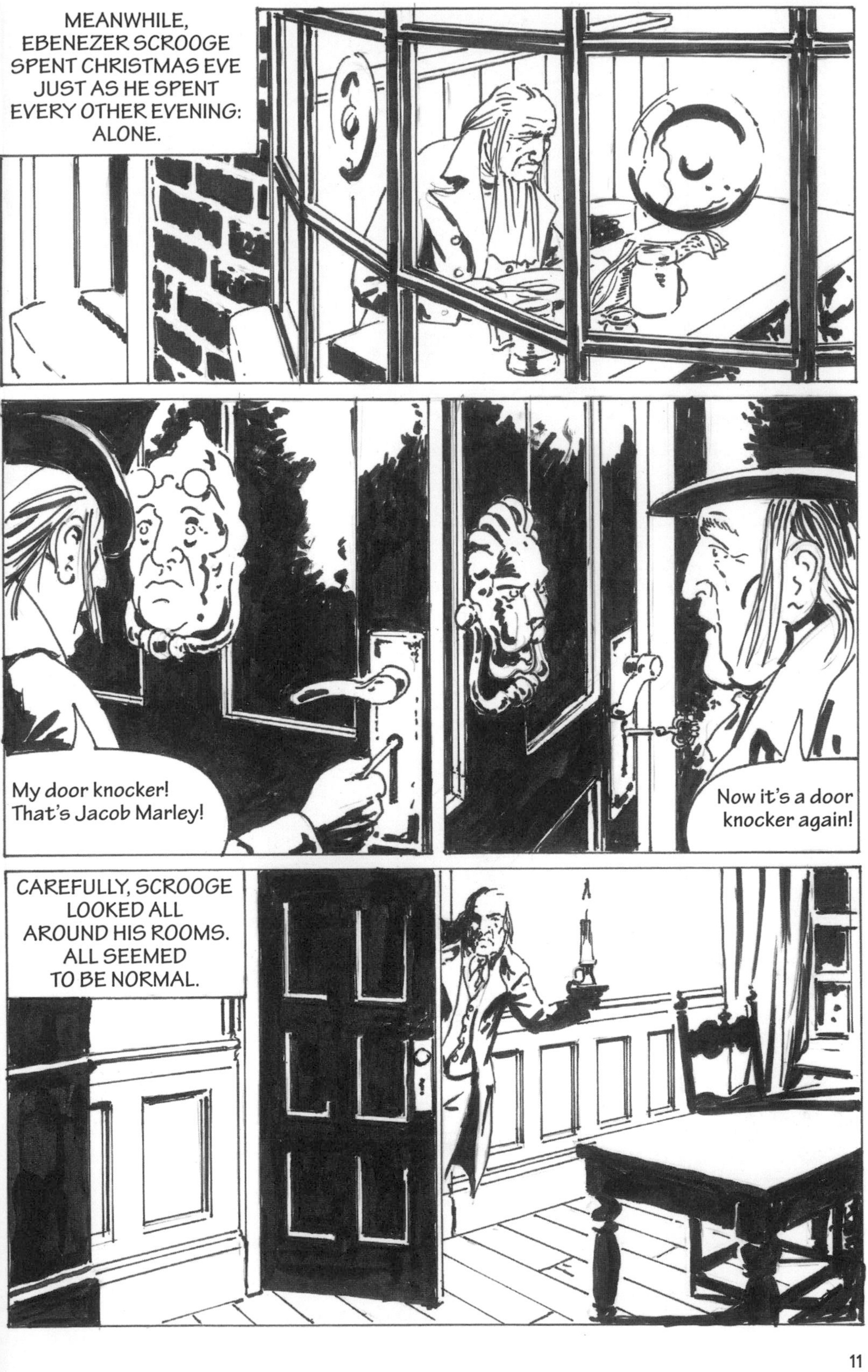
MEANWHILE, EBENEZER SCROOGE SPENT CHRISTMAS EVE JUST AS HE SPENT EVERY OTHER EVENING: ALONE.
My door knocker! That's Jacob Marley!
Now it's a door knocker again!
CAREFULLY, SCROOGE LOOKED ALL AROUND HIS ROOMS. ALL SEEMED TO BE NORMAL.

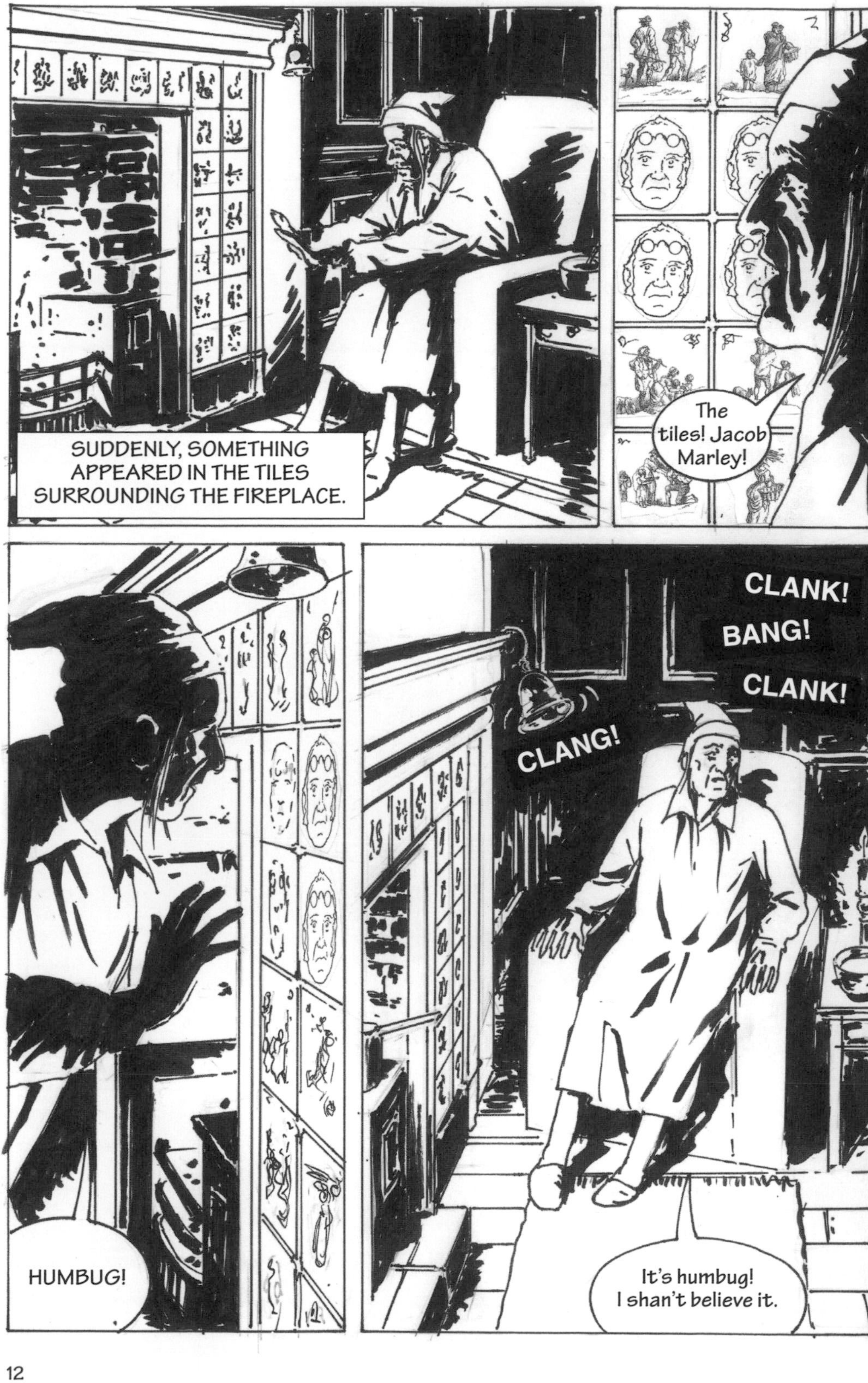
SUDDENLY, SOMETHING APPEARED IN THE TILES SURROUNDING THE FIREPLACE.
The tiles! Jacob Marley!
HUMBUG!
CLANK!
BANG!
CLANK!
CLANG!
It's humbug! I shan't believe it.

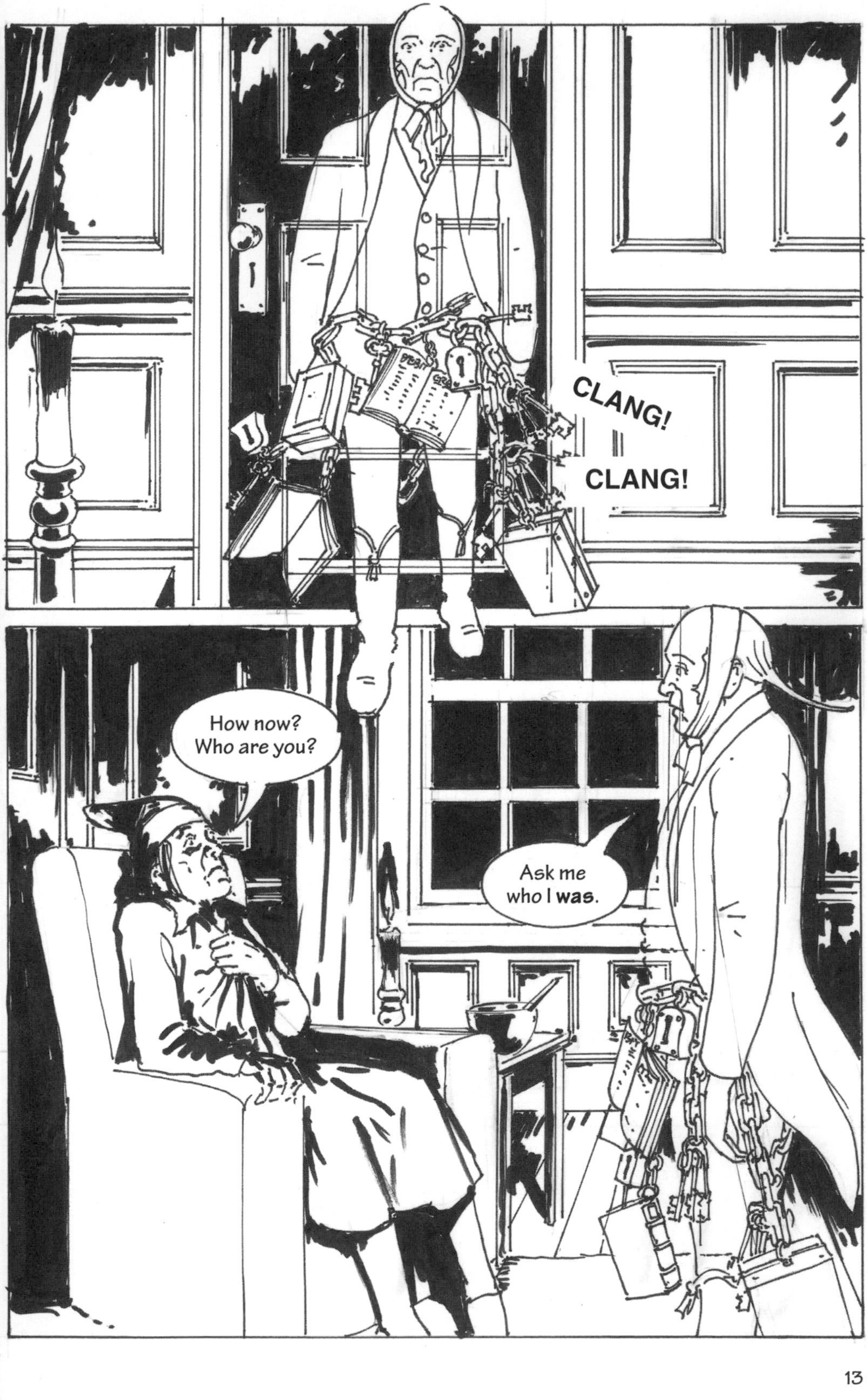
CLANG!
CLANG!
How now? Who are you?
Ask me who I was.

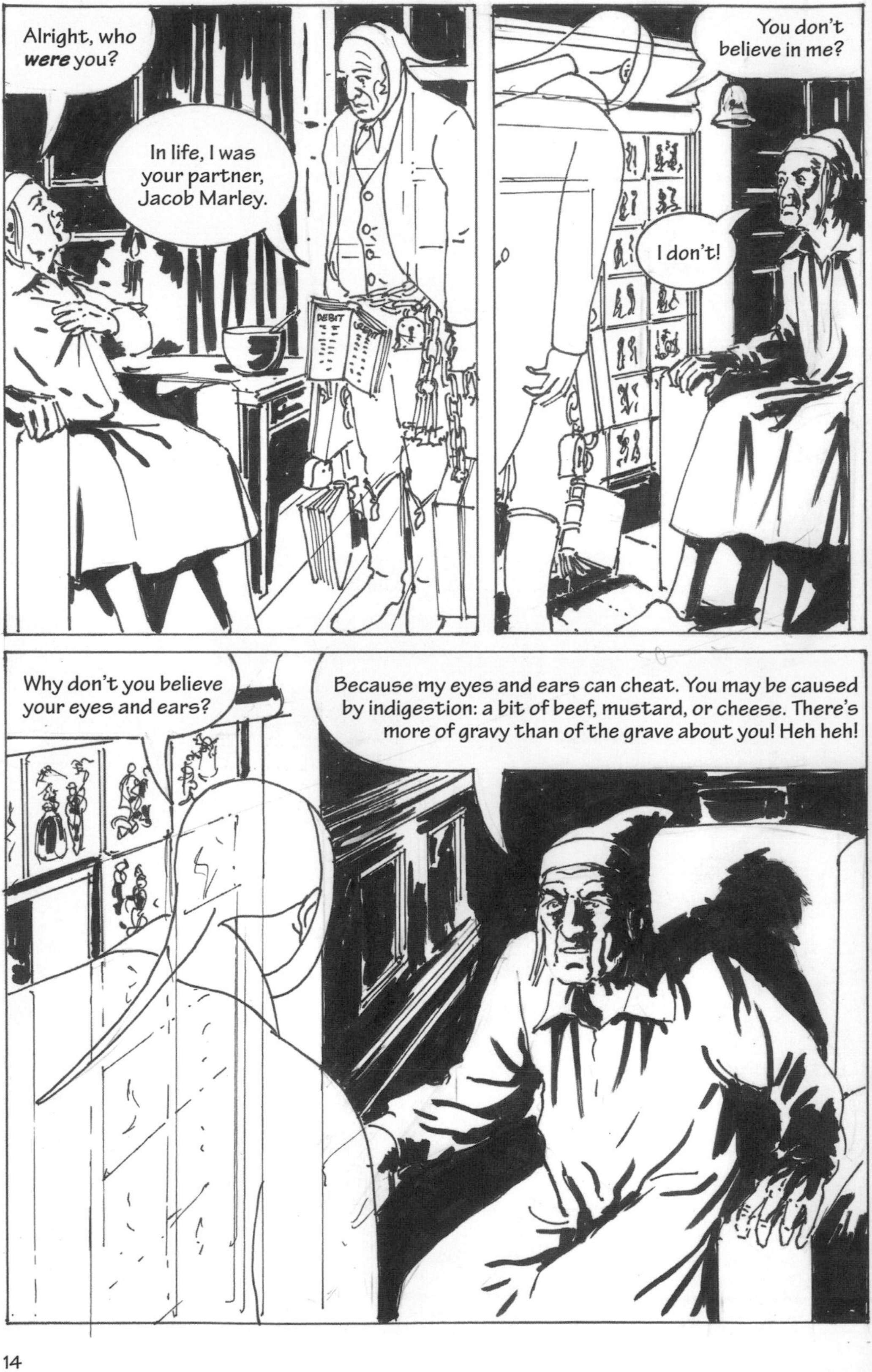
Alright, who *were* you?
In life, I was your partner, Jacob Marley.
DEBIT
CREDIT
You don't believe in me?
I don't!
Why don't you believe your eyes and ears?
Because my eyes and ears can cheat. You may be caused by indigestion: a bit of beef, mustard, or cheese. There's more of gravy than of the grave about you! Heh heh!

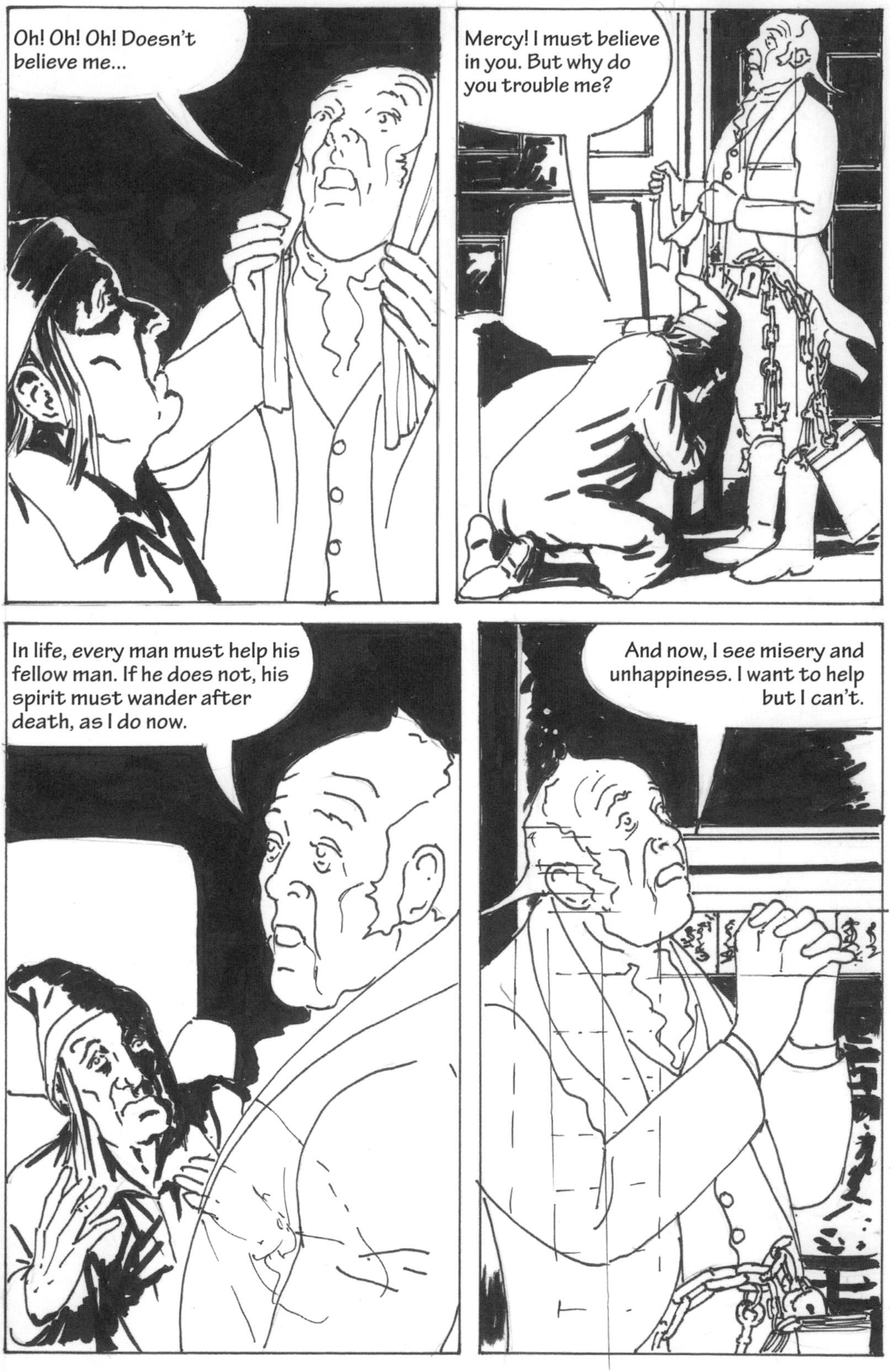
Oh! Oh! Oh! Doesn't believe me...
Mercy! I must believe in you. But why do you trouble me?
In life, every man must help his fellow man. If he does not, his spirit must wander after death, as I do now.
And now, I see misery and unhappiness. I want to help but I can't.

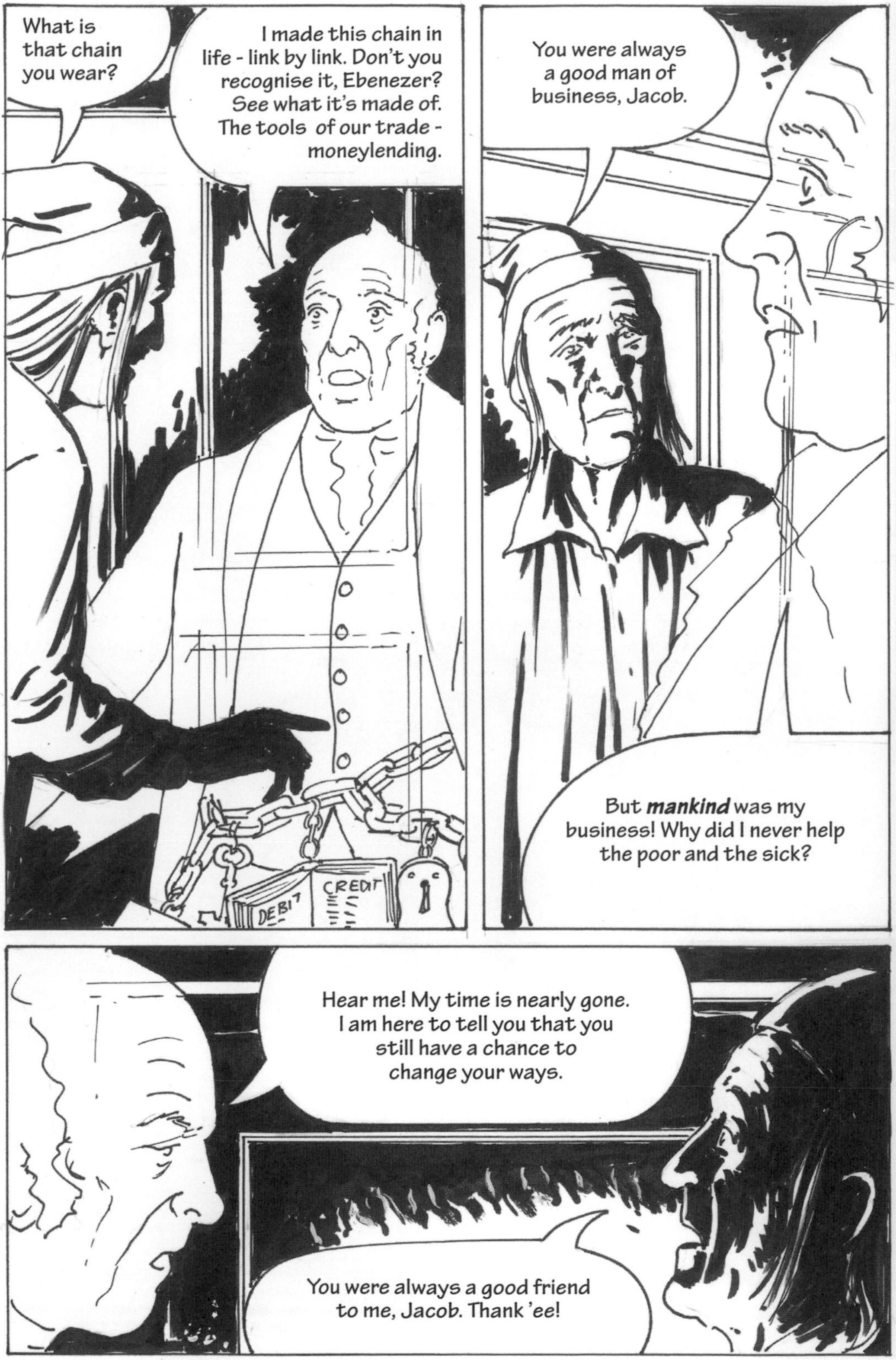
What is that chain you wear?
I made this chain in life - link by link. Don't you recognise it, Ebenezer? See what it's made of. The tools of our trade - moneylending.
DEBIT
CREDIT
You were always a good man of business, Jacob.
But **mankind** was my business! Why did I never help the poor and the sick?
Hear me! My time is nearly gone. I am here to tell you that you still have a chance to change your ways.
You were always a good friend to me, Jacob. Thank 'ee!

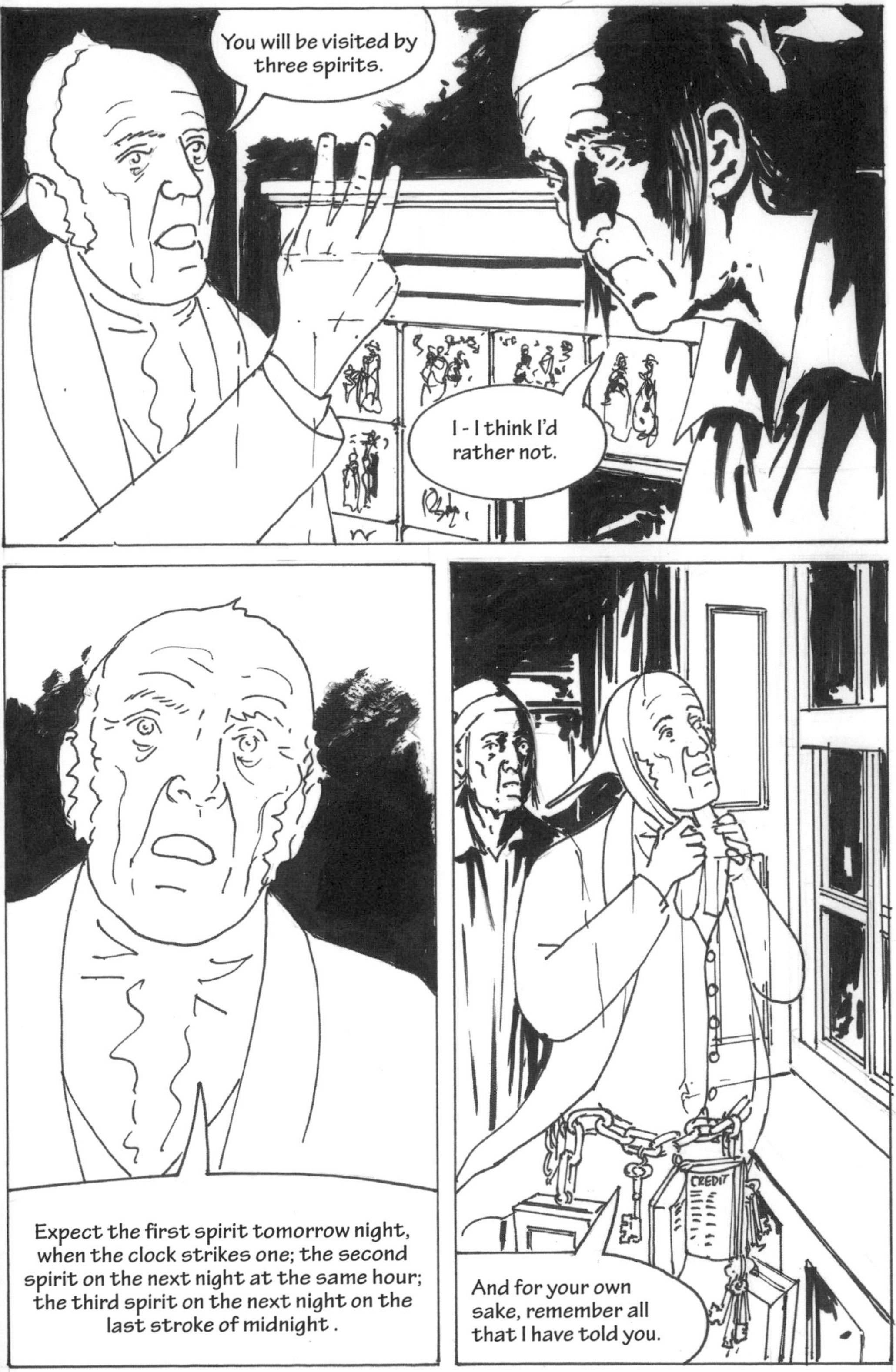
You will be visited by three spirits.
I - I think I'd rather not.
Expect the first spirit tomorrow night, when the clock strikes one; the second spirit on the next night at the same hour; the third spirit on the next night on the last stroke of midnight .
CREDIT
And for your own sake, remember all that I have told you.

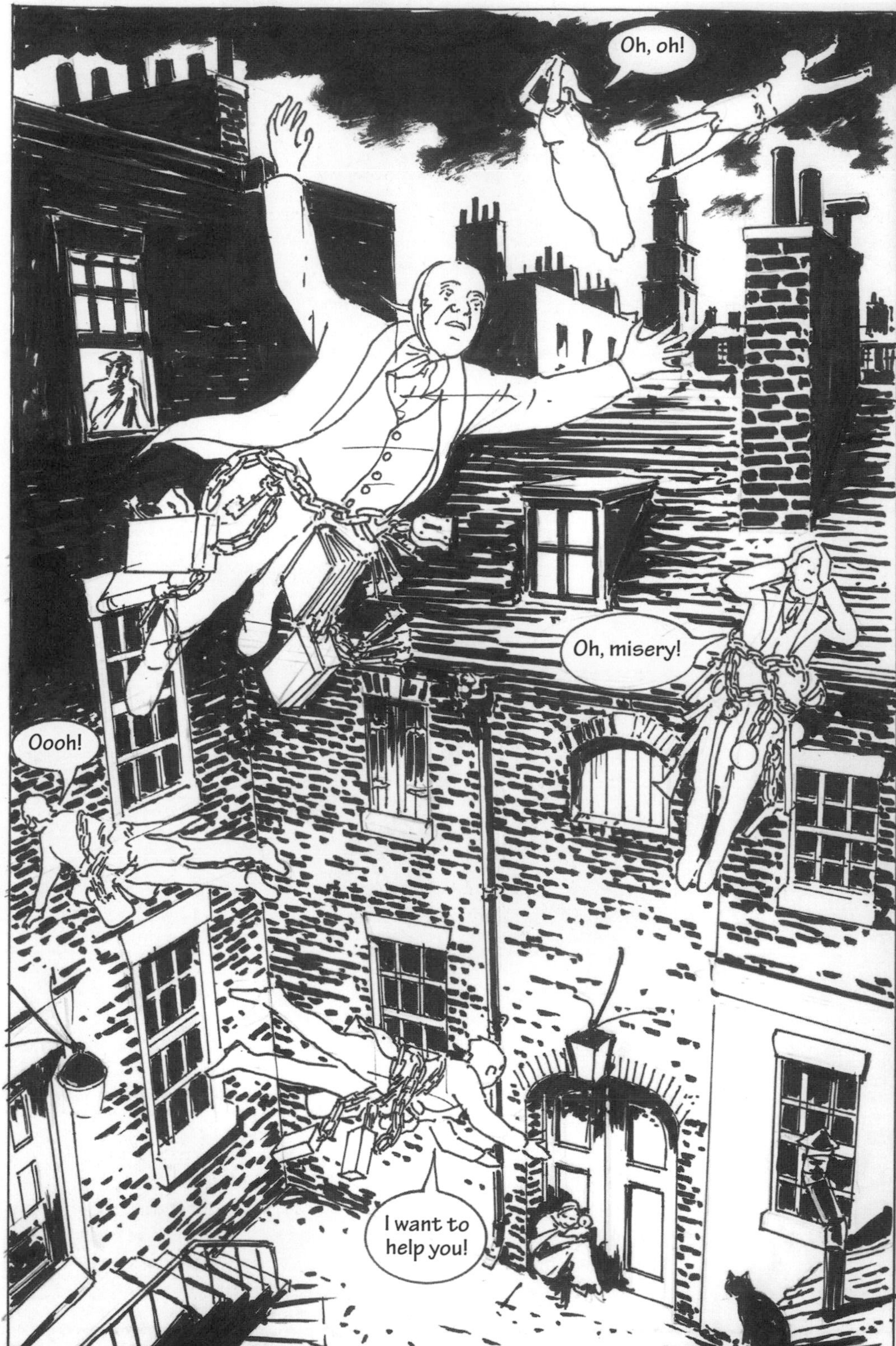
Oh, oh!
Oh, misery!
Oooh!
I want to help you!

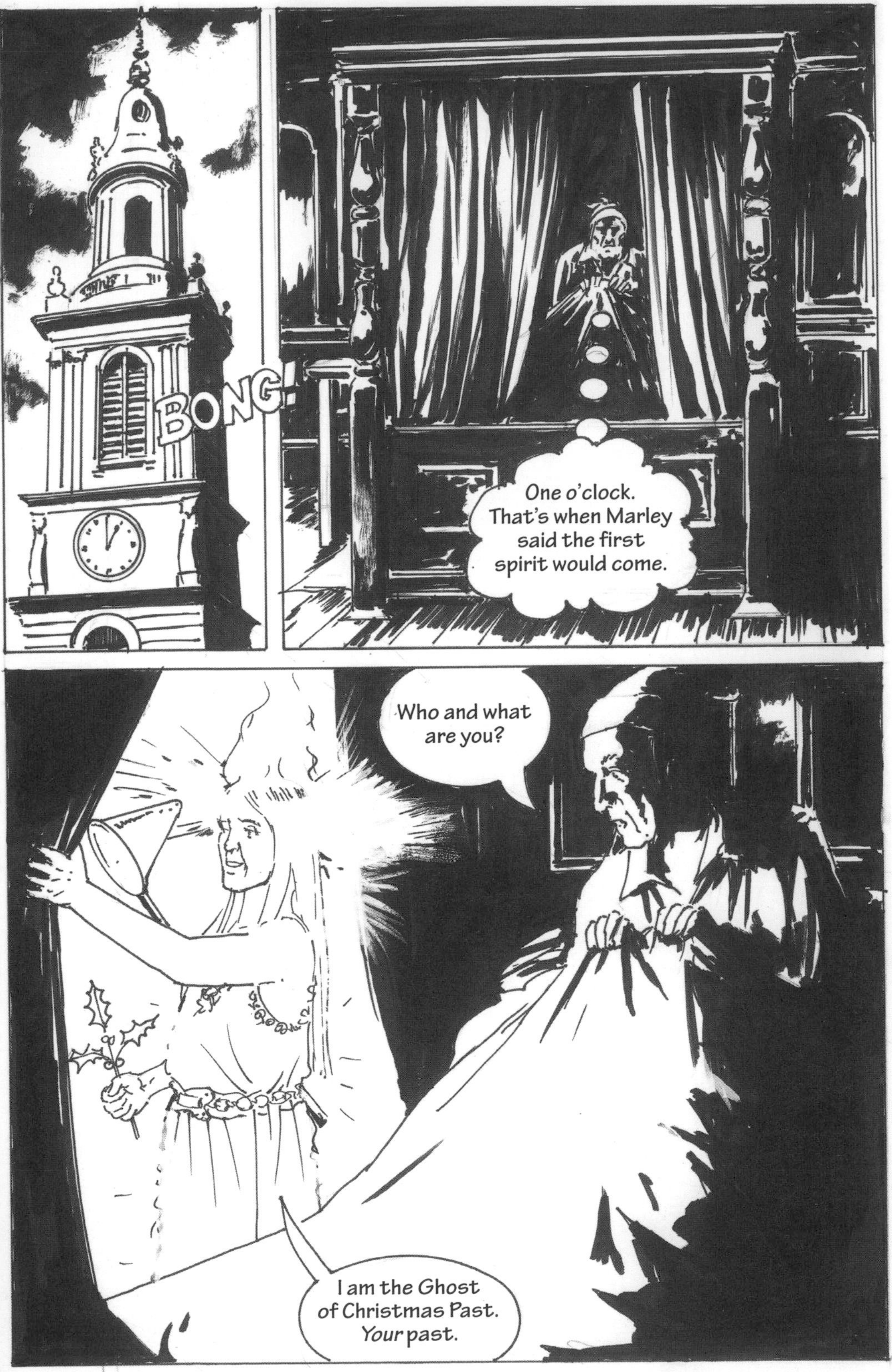
BONG!
One o'clock. That's when Marley said the first spirit would come.
Who and what are you?
I am the Ghost of Christmas Past. *Your* past.

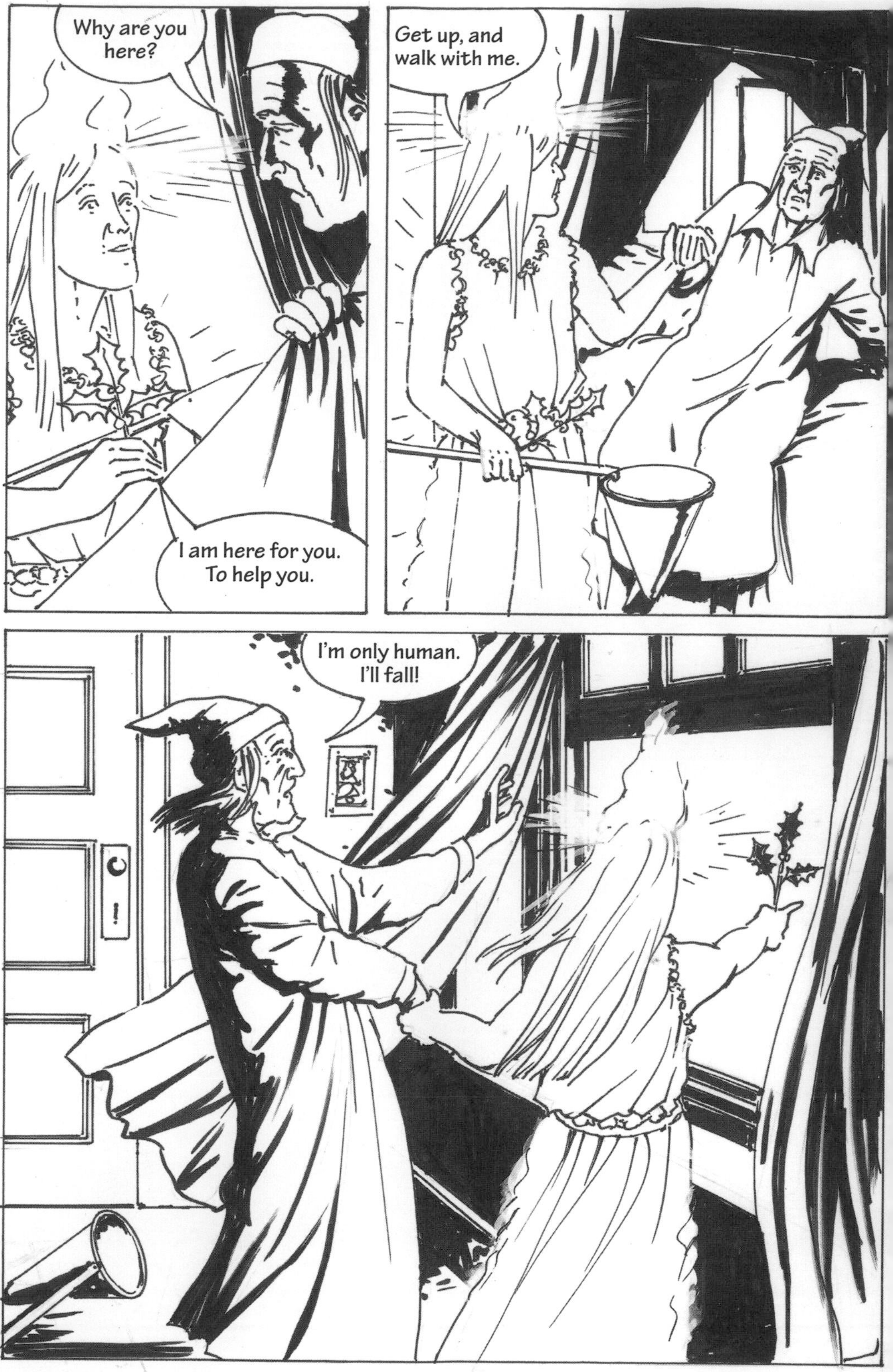
Why are you here?
I am here for you. To help you.
Get up, and walk with me.
I'm only human. I'll fall!

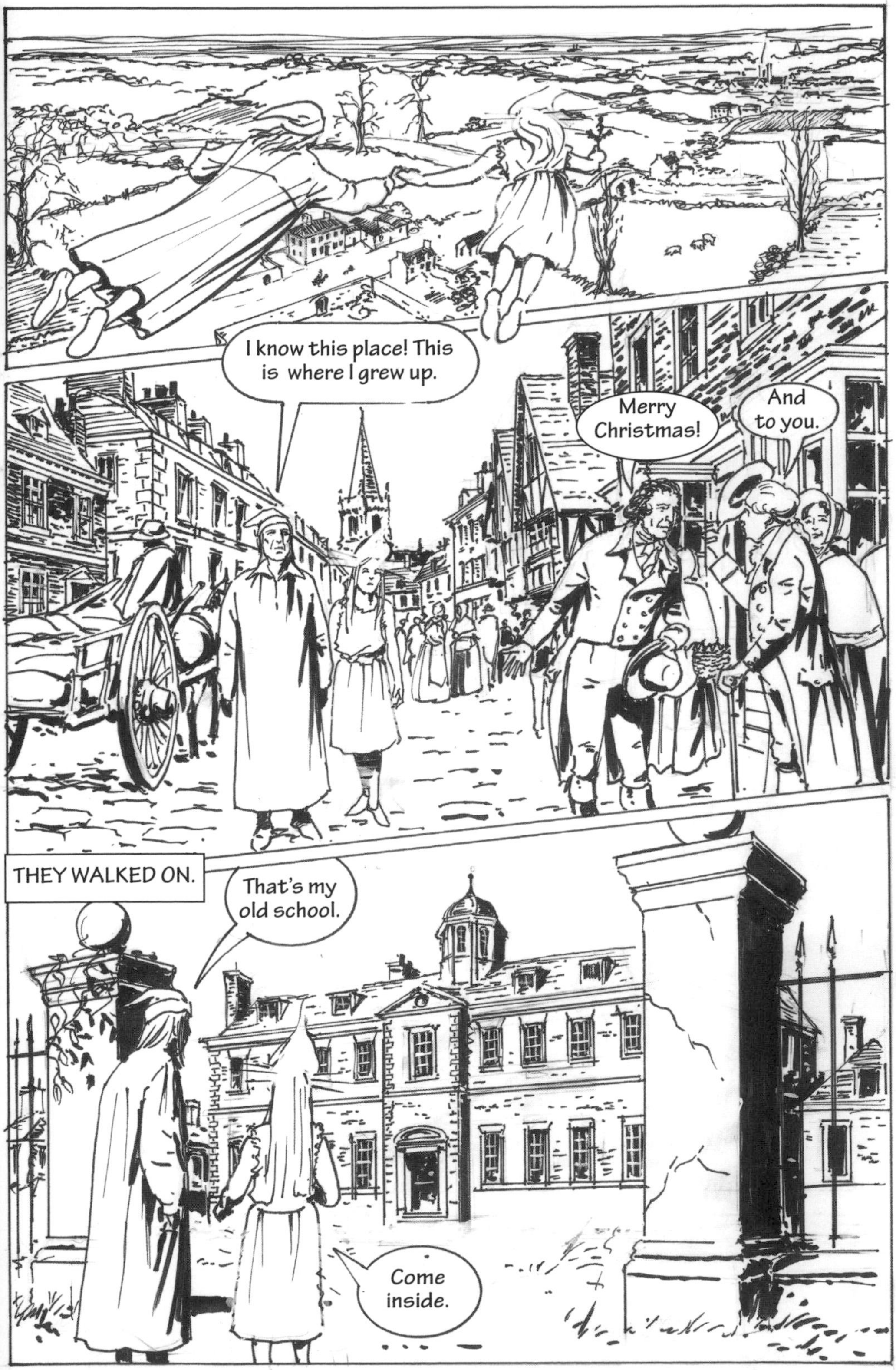
I know this place! This is where I grew up.
Merry Christmas!
And to you.
THEY WALKED ON.
That's my old school.
Come inside.

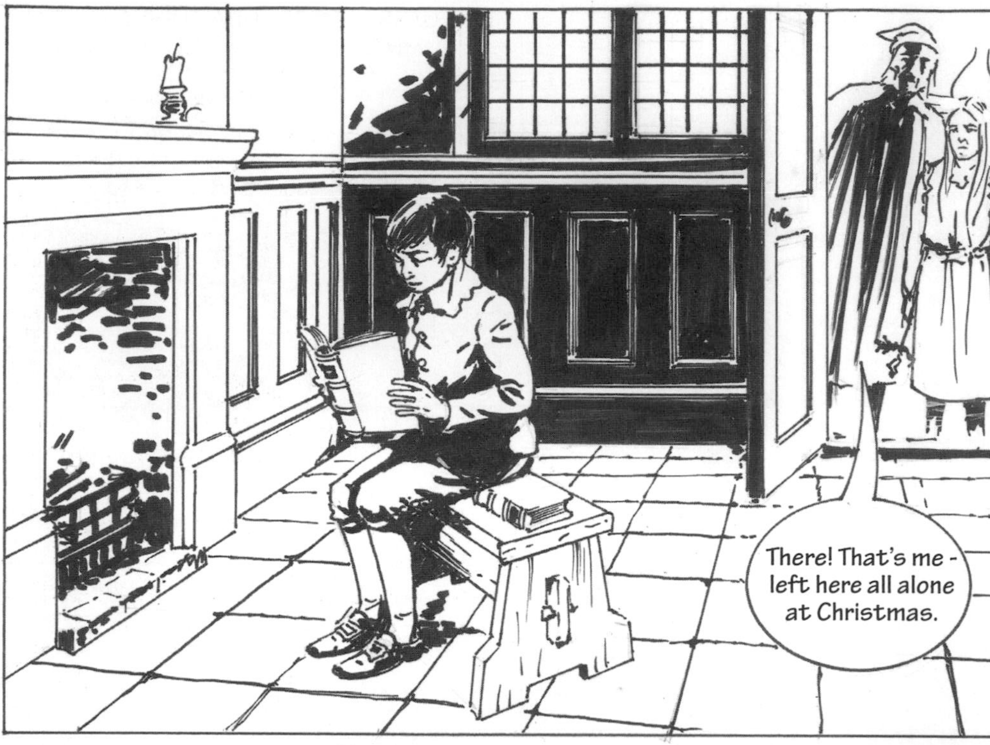
There! That's me - left here all alone at Christmas.

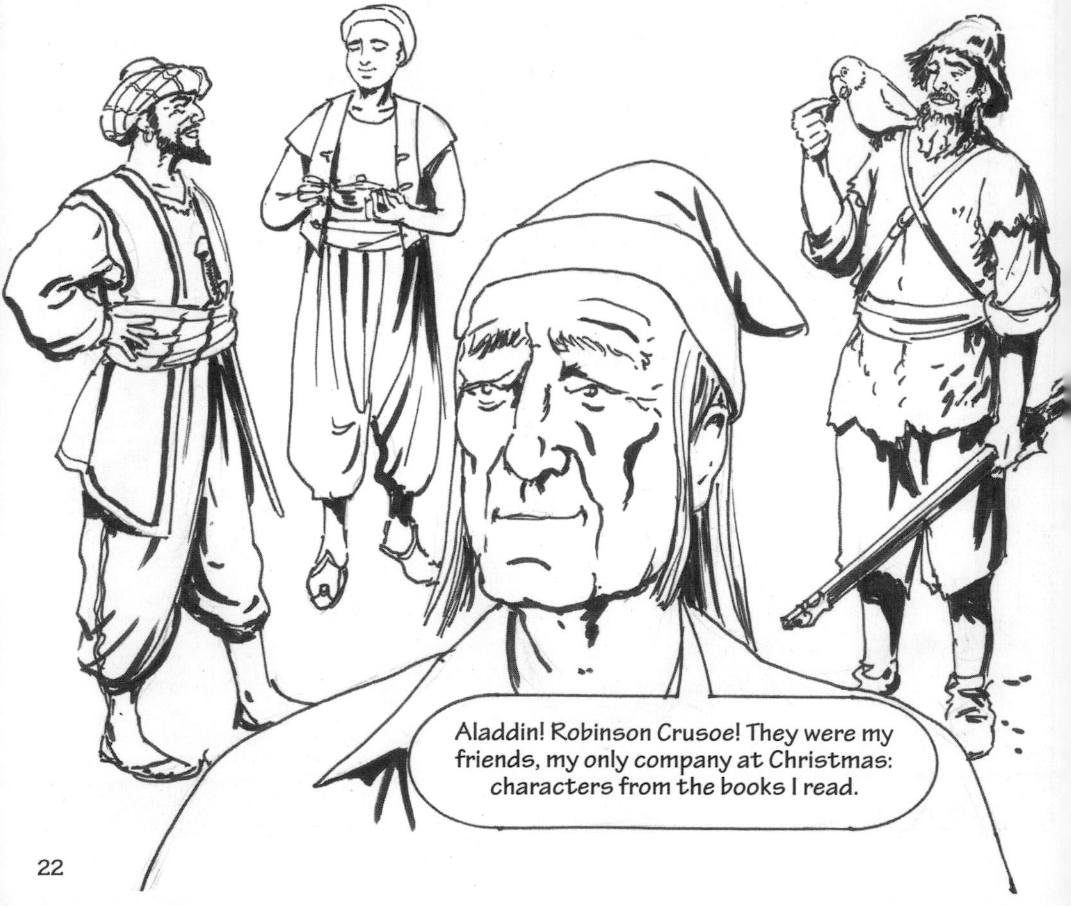
Aladdin! Robinson Crusoe! They were my friends, my only company at Christmas: characters from the books I read.

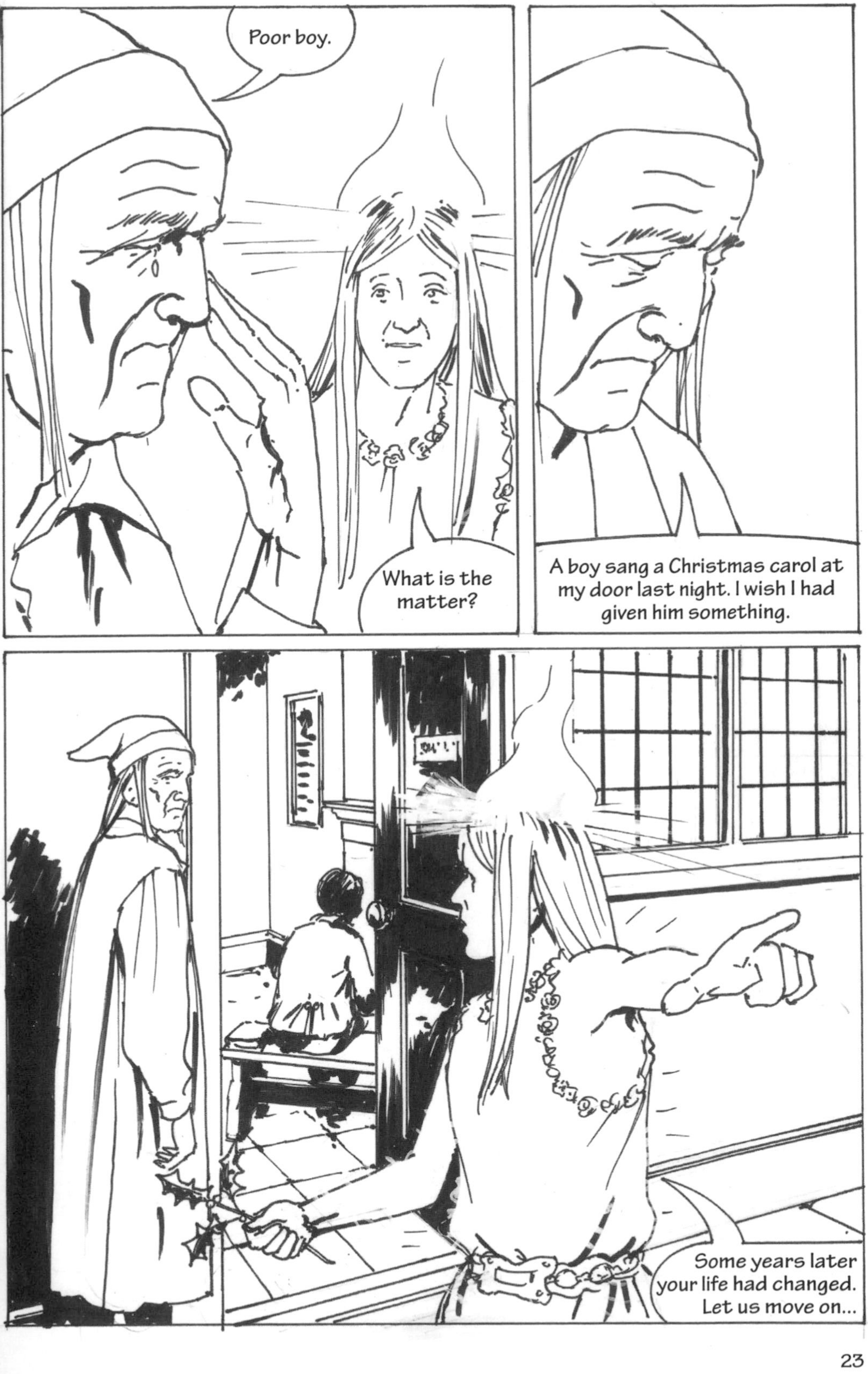
Poor boy.
What is the matter?
A boy sang a Christmas carol at my door last night. I wish I had given him something.
Some years later your life had changed. Let us move on...

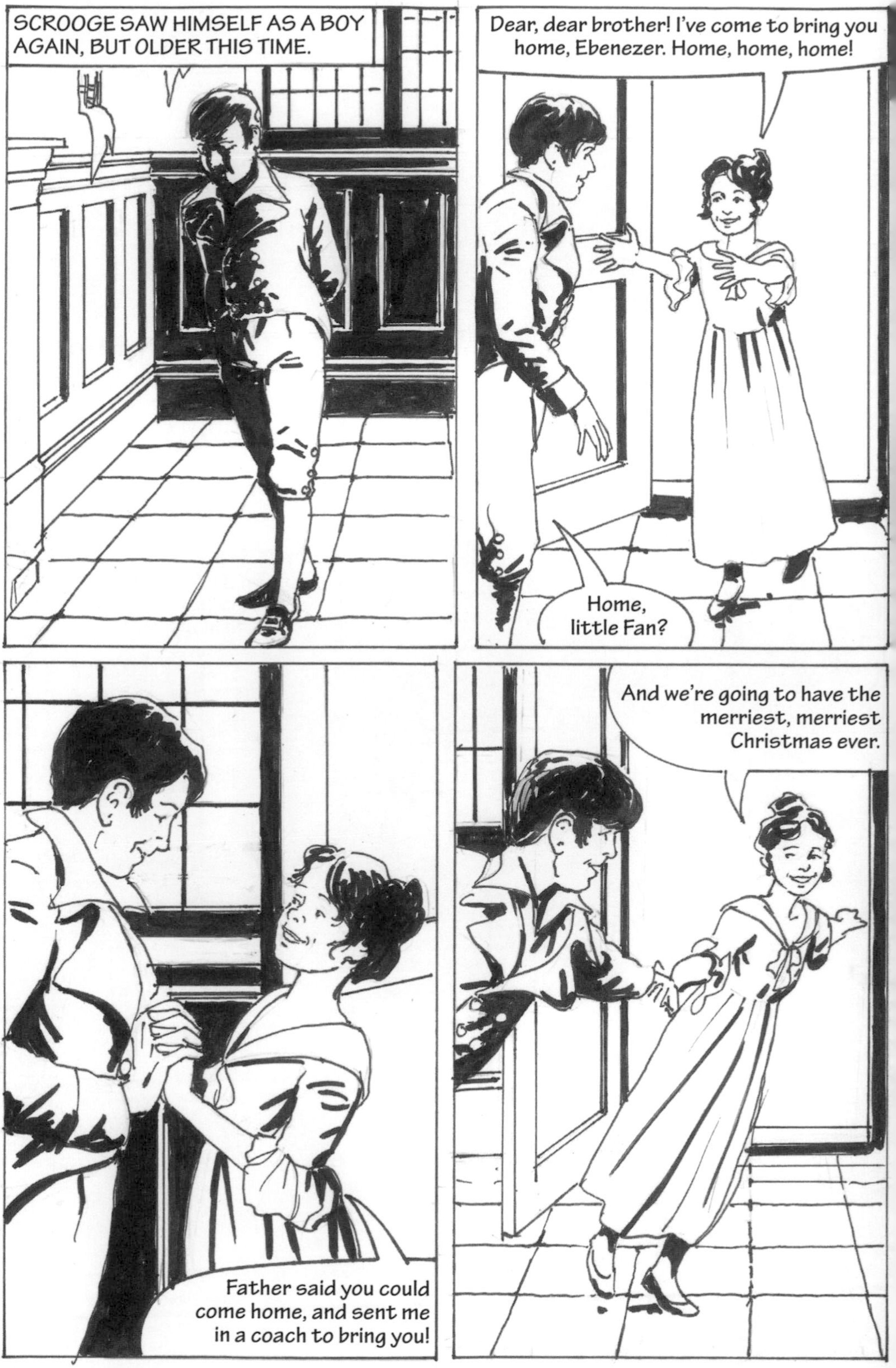
SCROOGE SAW HIMSELF AS A BOY AGAIN, BUT OLDER THIS TIME.
Dear, dear brother! I've come to bring you home, Ebenezer. Home, home, home!
Home, little Fan?
Father said you could come home, and sent me in a coach to bring you!
And we're going to have the merriest, merriest Christmas ever.

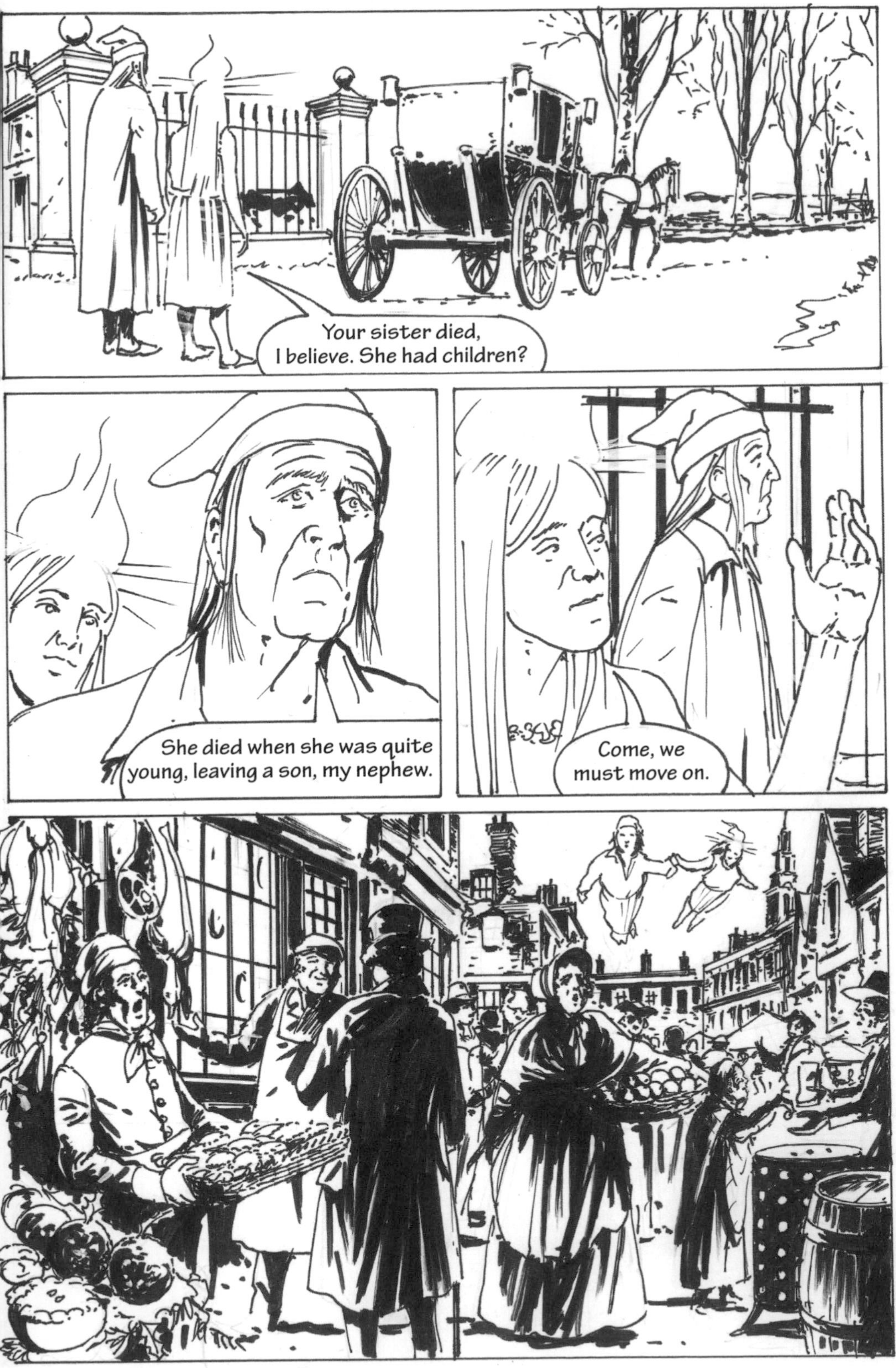
Your sister died,
I believe. She had children?
She died when she was quite
young, leaving a son, my nephew.
Come, we
must move on.

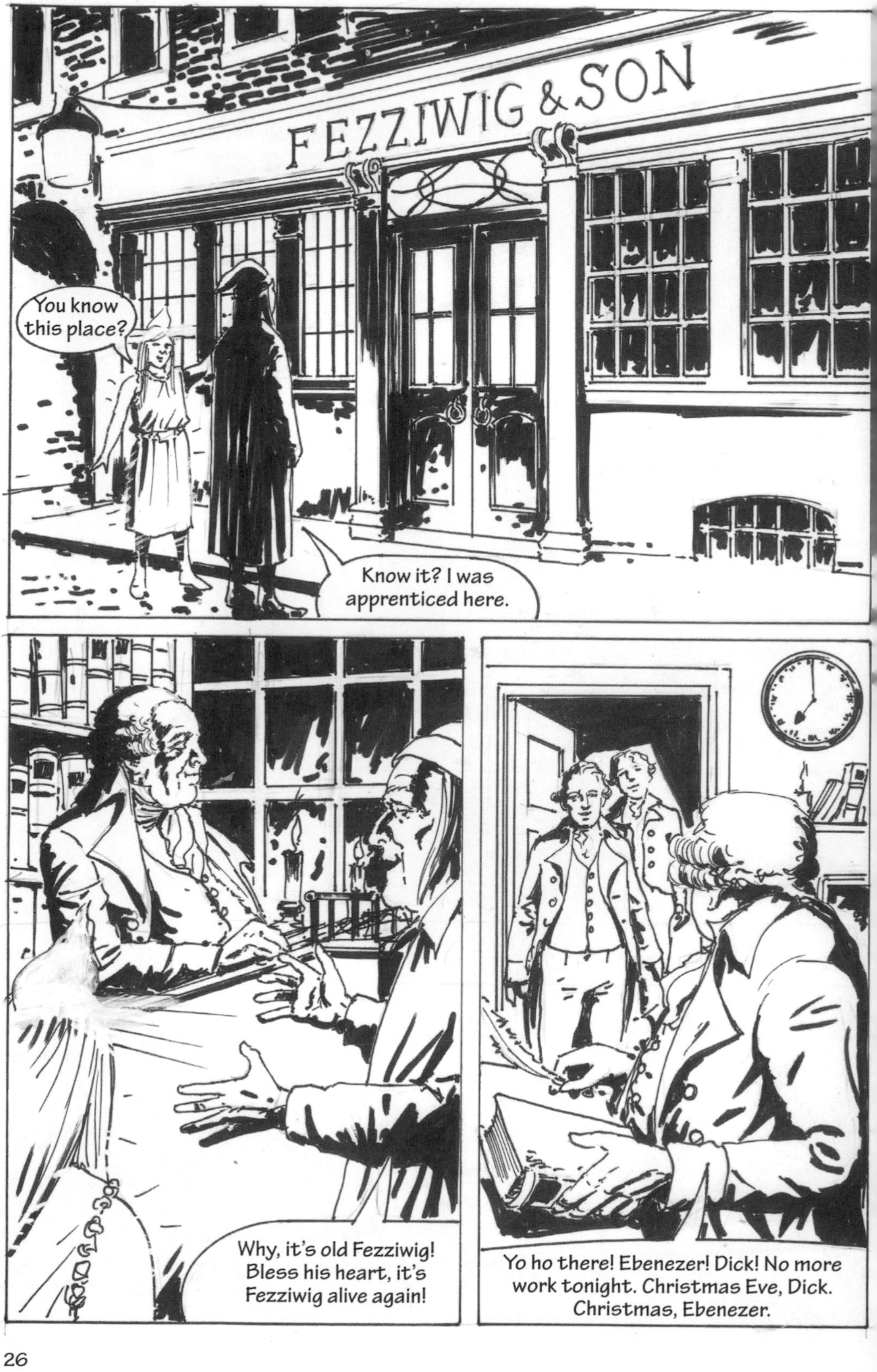
FEZZIWIG & SON
You know this place?
Know it? I was apprenticed here.
Why, it's old Fezziwig! Bless his heart, it's Fezziwig alive again!
Yo ho there! Ebenezer! Dick! No more work tonight. Christmas Eve, Dick. Christmas, Ebenezer.

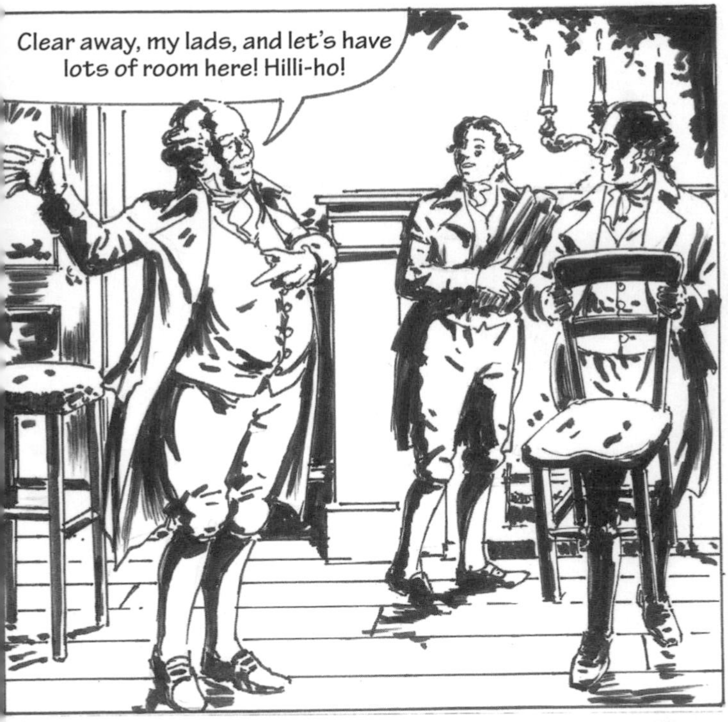
Clear away, my lads, and let's have lots of room here! Hilli-ho!

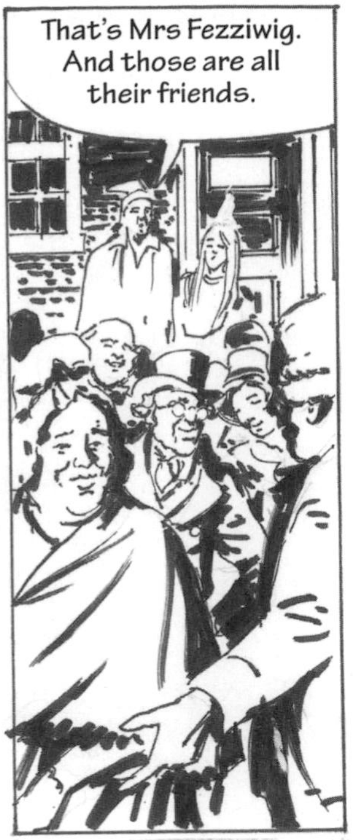
That's Mrs Fezziwig. And those are all their friends.

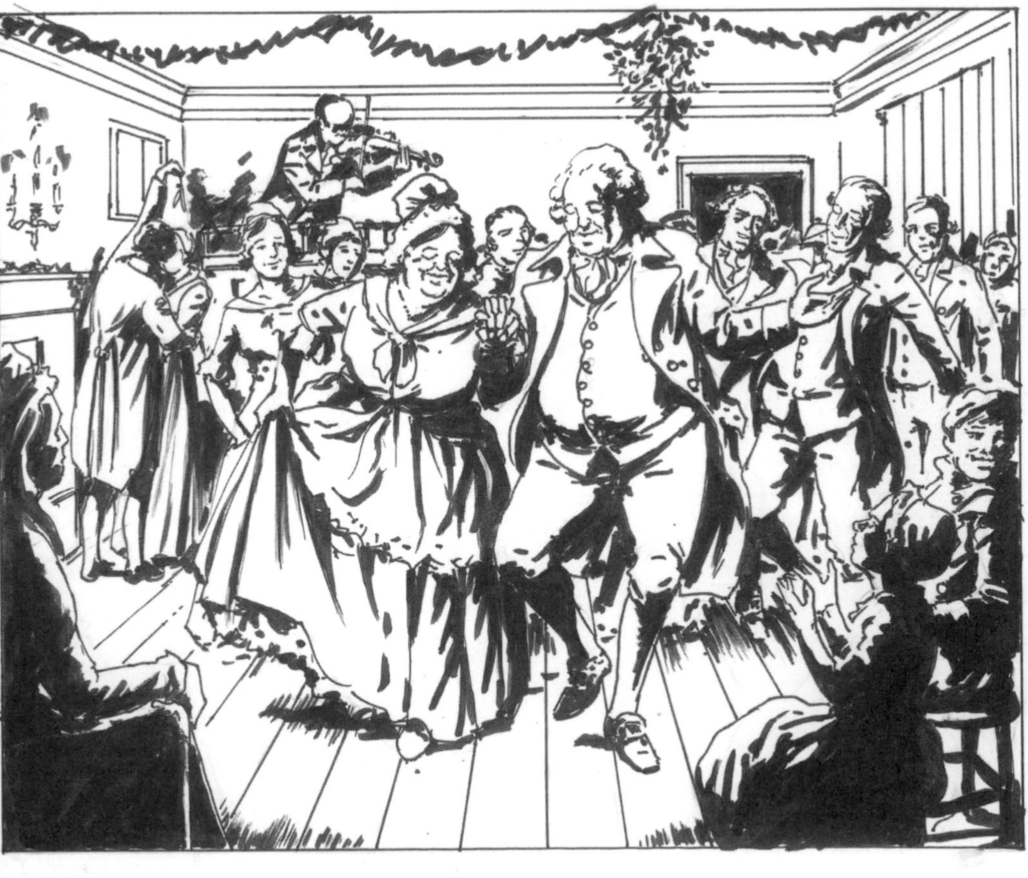

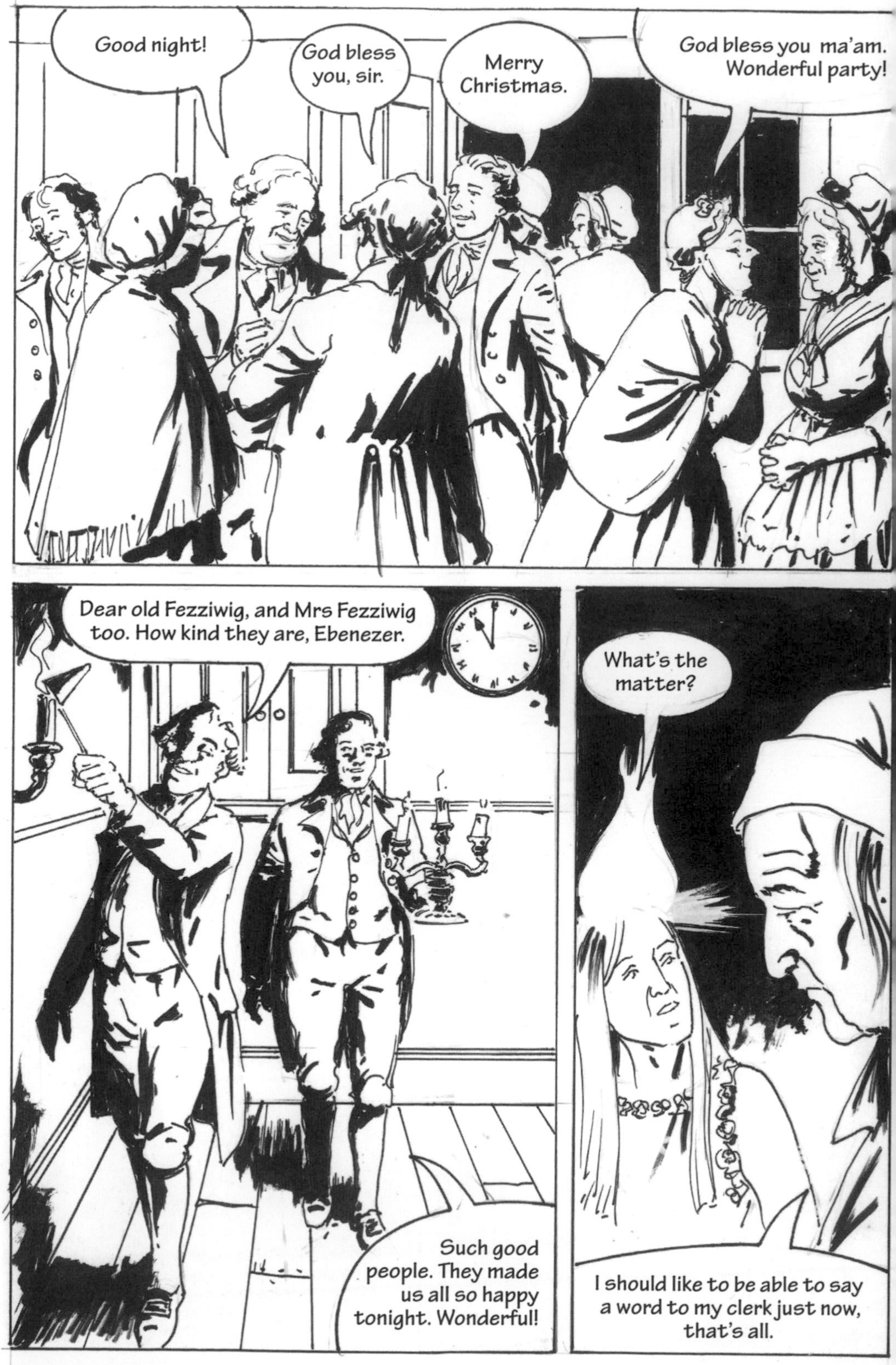
Good night!
God bless you, sir.
Merry Christmas.
God bless you ma'am. Wonderful party!
Dear old Fezziwig, and Mrs Fezziwig too. How kind they are, Ebenezer.
Such good people. They made us all so happy tonight. Wonderful!
What's the matter?
I should like to be able to say a word to my clerk just now, that's all.

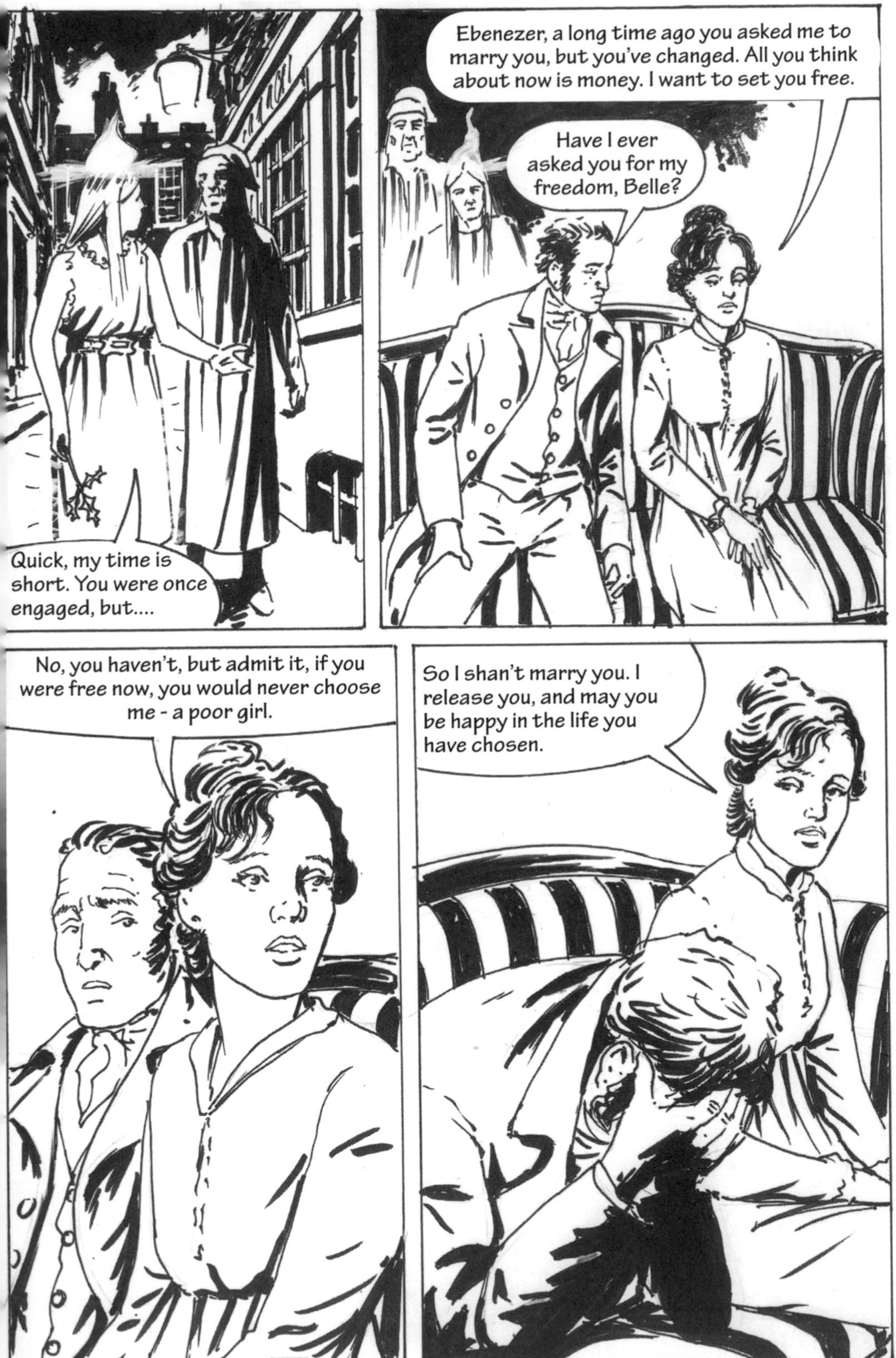
Quick, my time is short. You were once engaged, but....
Ebenezer, a long time ago you asked me to marry you, but you've changed. All you think about now is money. I want to set you free.
Have I ever asked you for my freedom, Belle?
No, you haven't, but admit it, if you were free now, you would never choose me - a poor girl.
So I shan't marry you. I release you, and may you be happy in the life you have chosen.

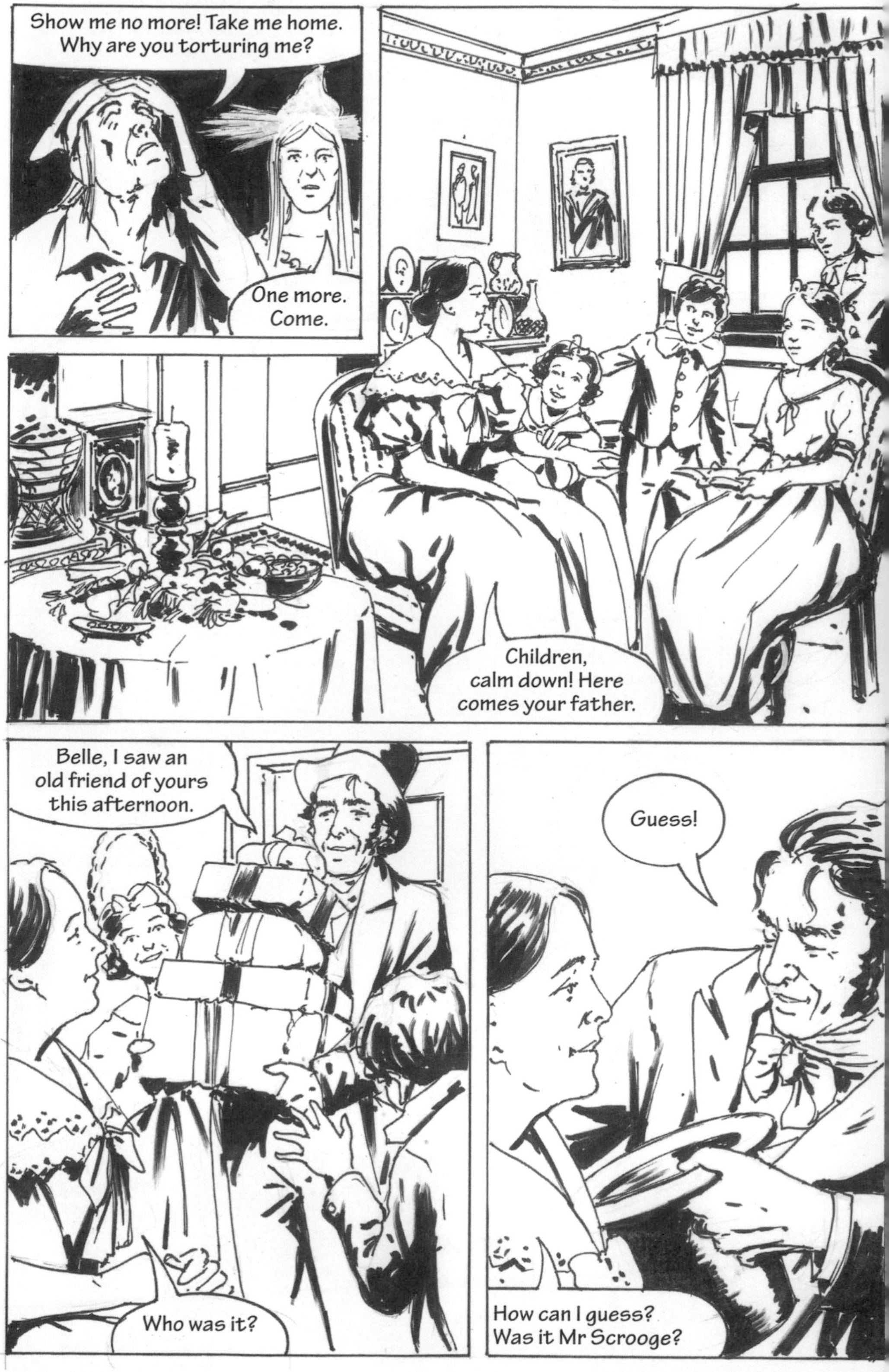
Show me no more! Take me home. Why are you torturing me?
One more. Come.
Children, calm down! Here comes your father.
Belle, I saw an old friend of yours this afternoon.
Who was it?
Guess!
How can I guess? Was it Mr Scrooge?

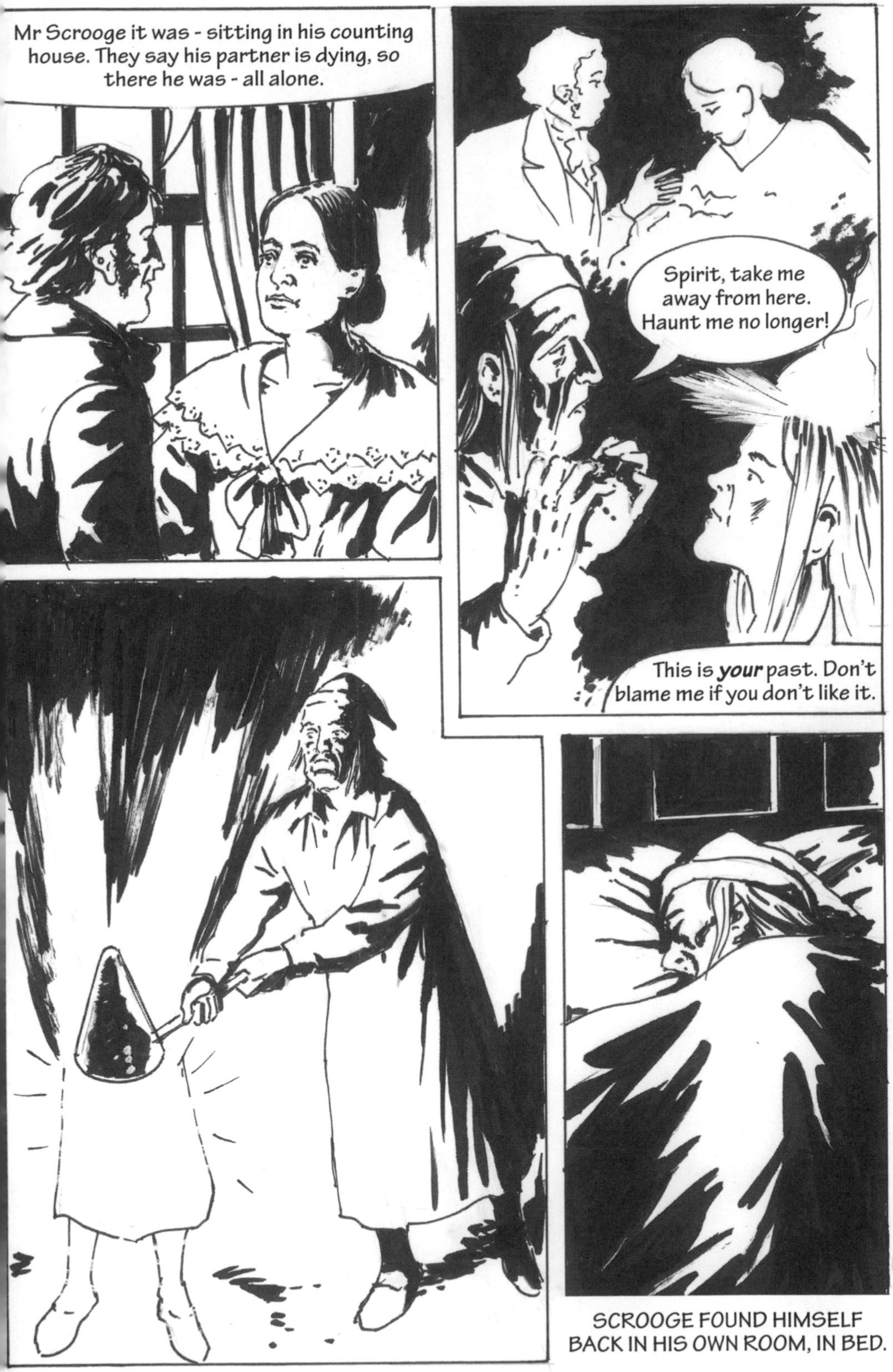
Mr Scrooge it was - sitting in his counting house. They say his partner is dying, so there he was - all alone.
Spirit, take me away from here. Haunt me no longer!
This is *your* past. Don't blame me if you don't like it.
SCROOGE FOUND HIMSELF BACK IN HIS OWN ROOM, IN BED.

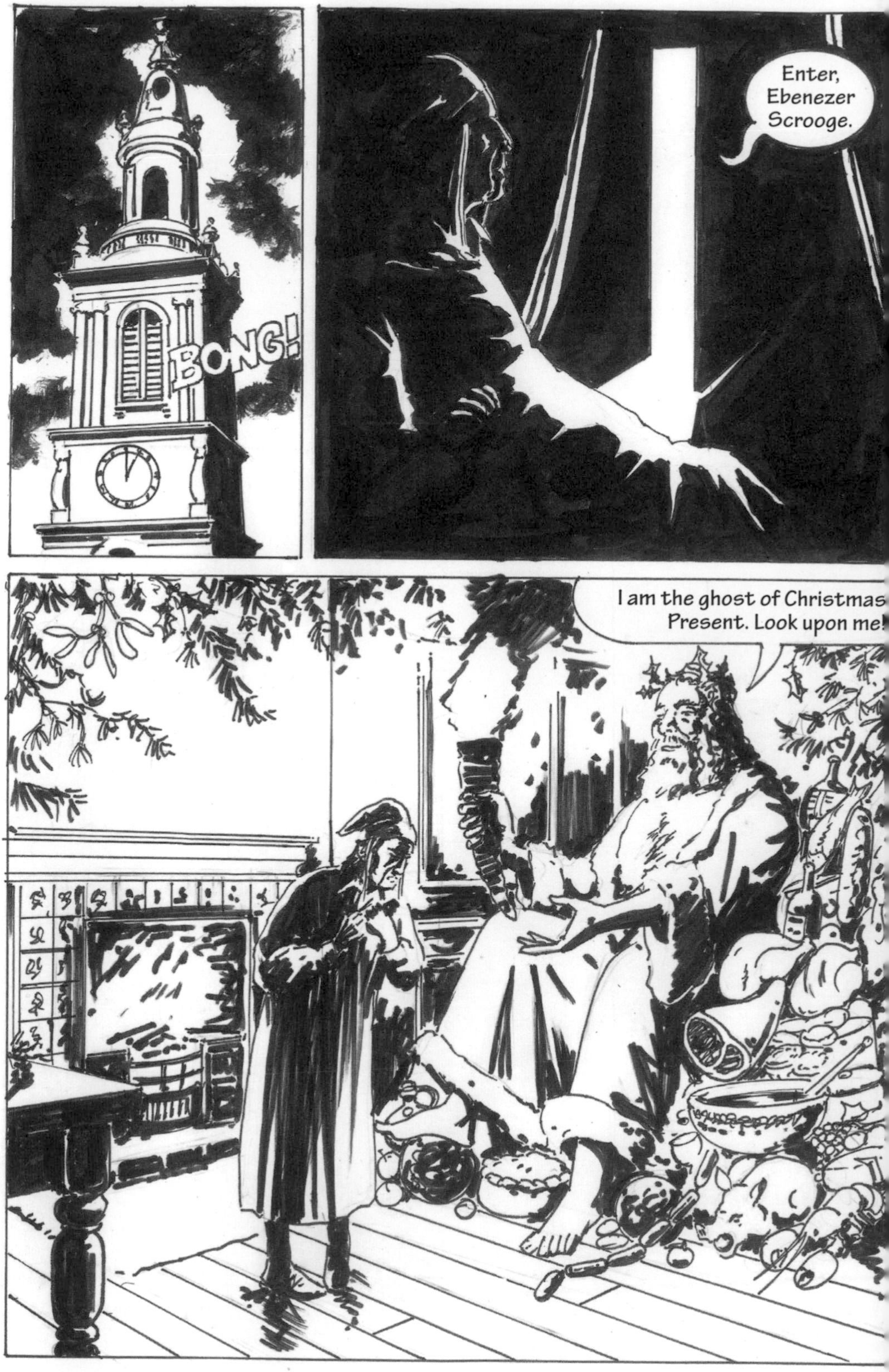
BONG!
Enter, Ebenezer Scrooge.
I am the ghost of Christmas Present. Look upon me!

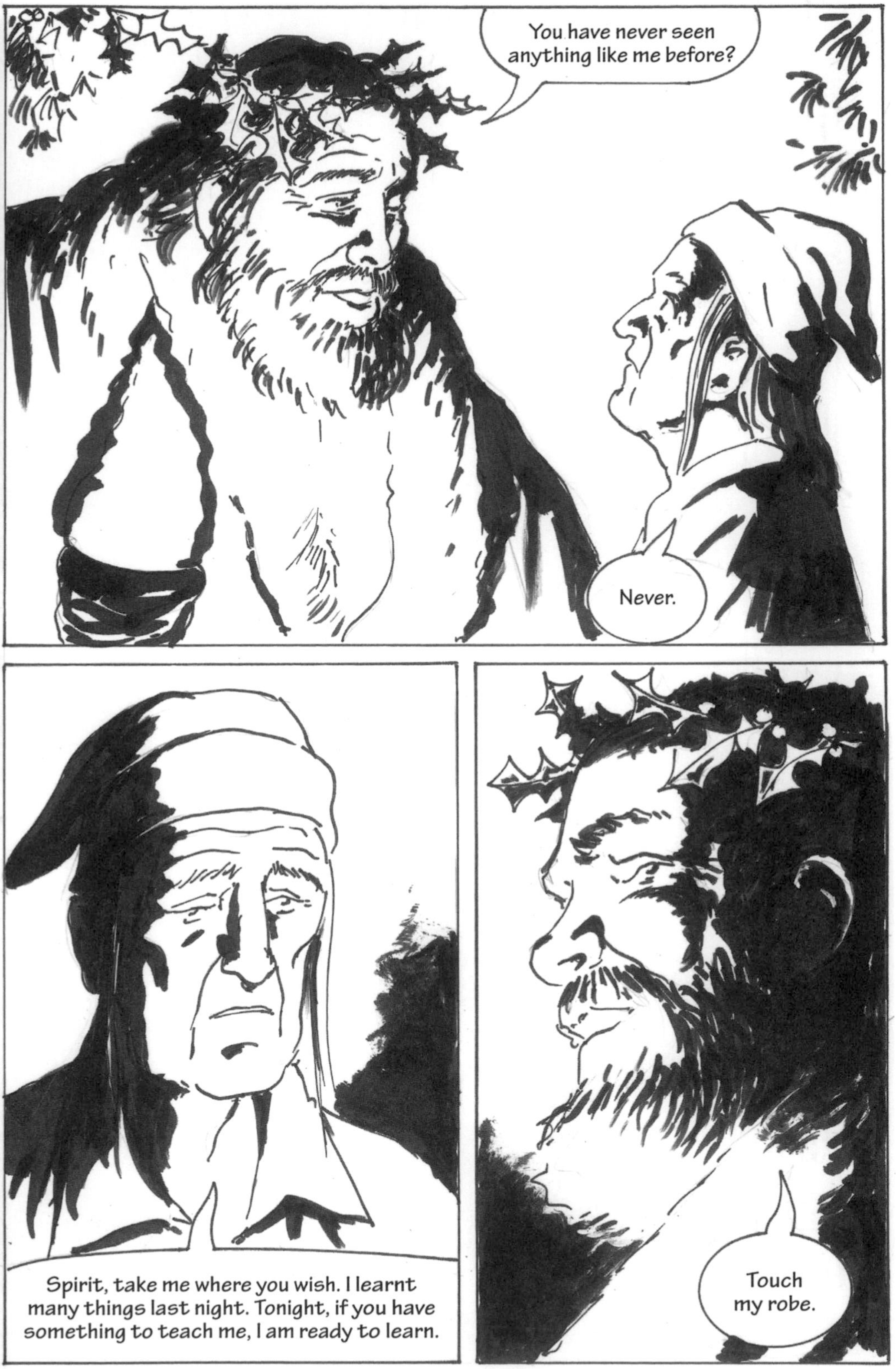
You have never seen anything like me before?
Never.
Spirit, take me where you wish. I learnt many things last night. Tonight, if you have something to teach me, I am ready to learn.
Touch my robe.

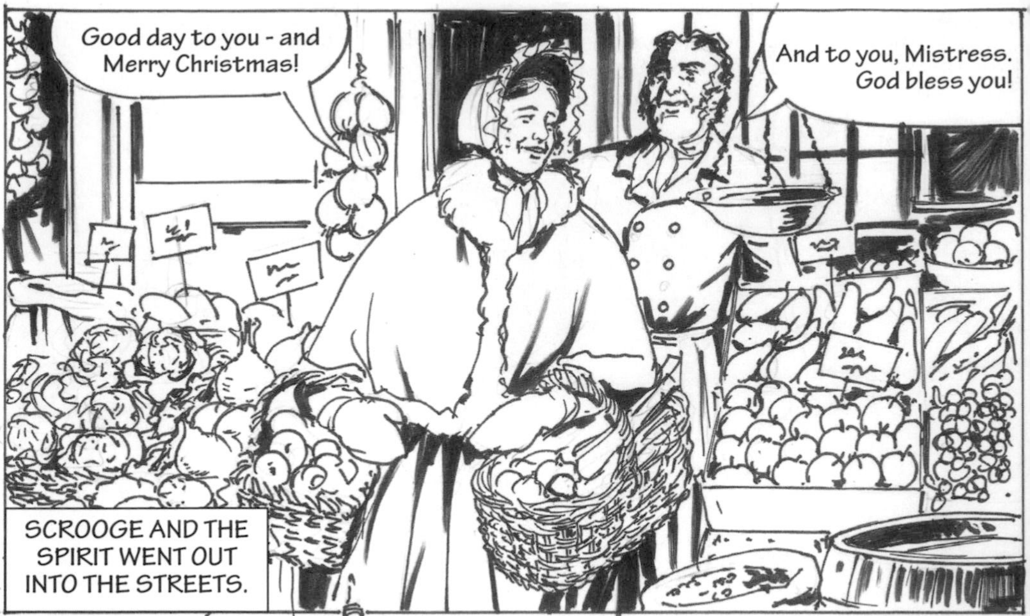
Good day to you - and Merry Christmas!
And to you, Mistress. God bless you!
SCROOGE AND THE SPIRIT WENT OUT INTO THE STREETS.

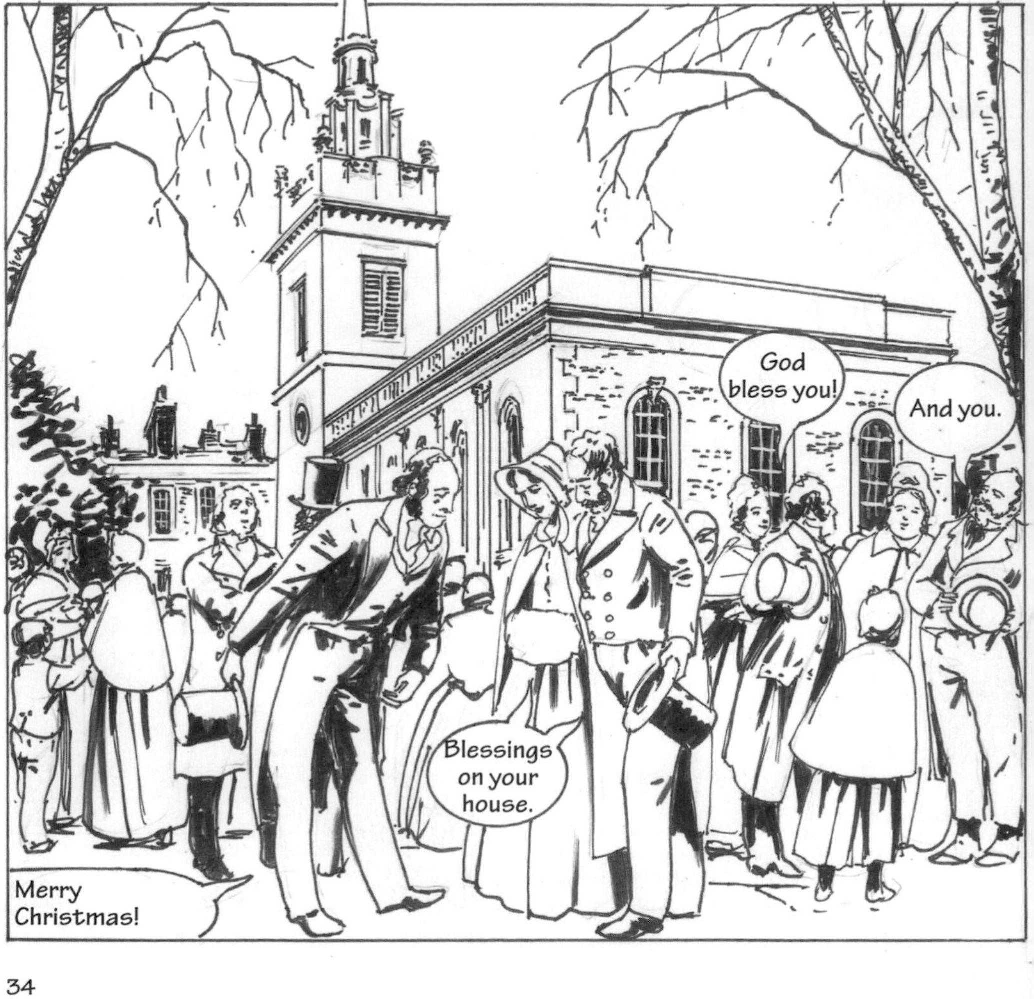
God bless you!
And you.
Blessings on your house.
Merry Christmas!

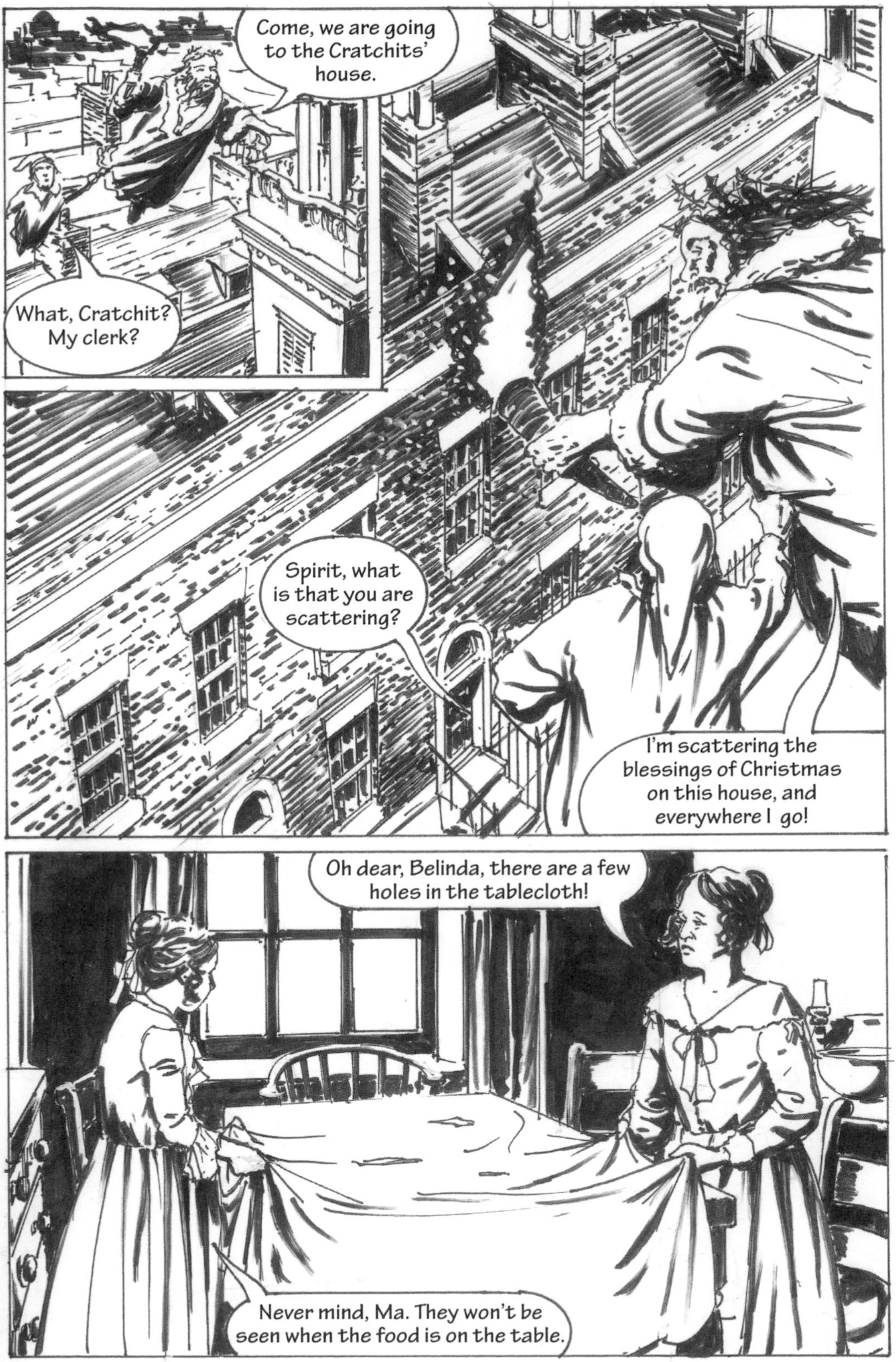
Come, we are going to the Cratchits' house.
What, Cratchit? My clerk?
Spirit, what is that you are scattering?
I'm scattering the blessings of Christmas on this house, and everywhere I go!
Oh dear, Belinda, there are a few holes in the tablecloth!
Never mind, Ma. They won't be seen when the food is on the table.

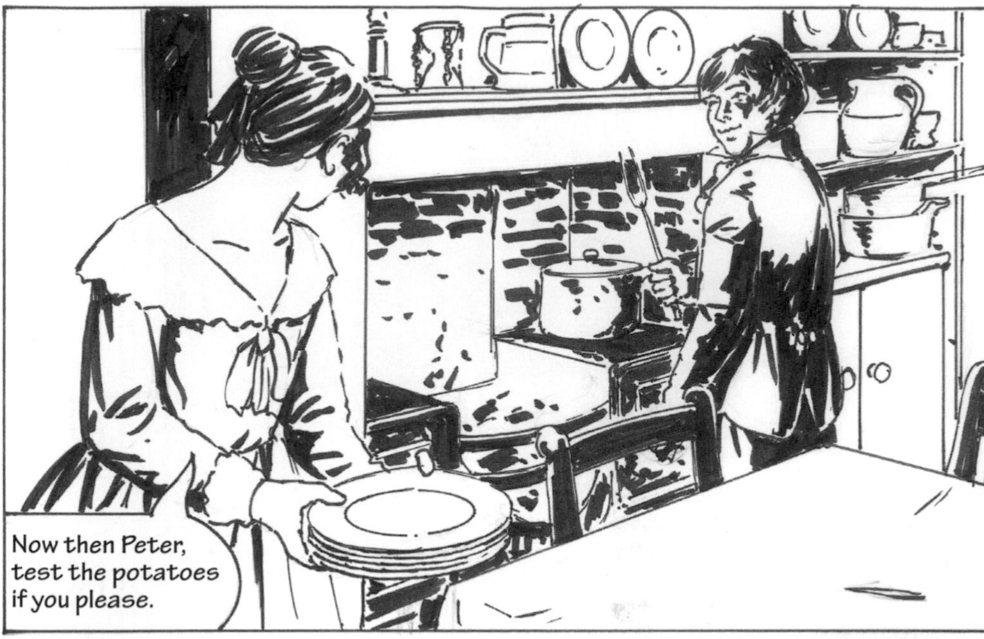
Now then Peter, test the potatoes if you please.

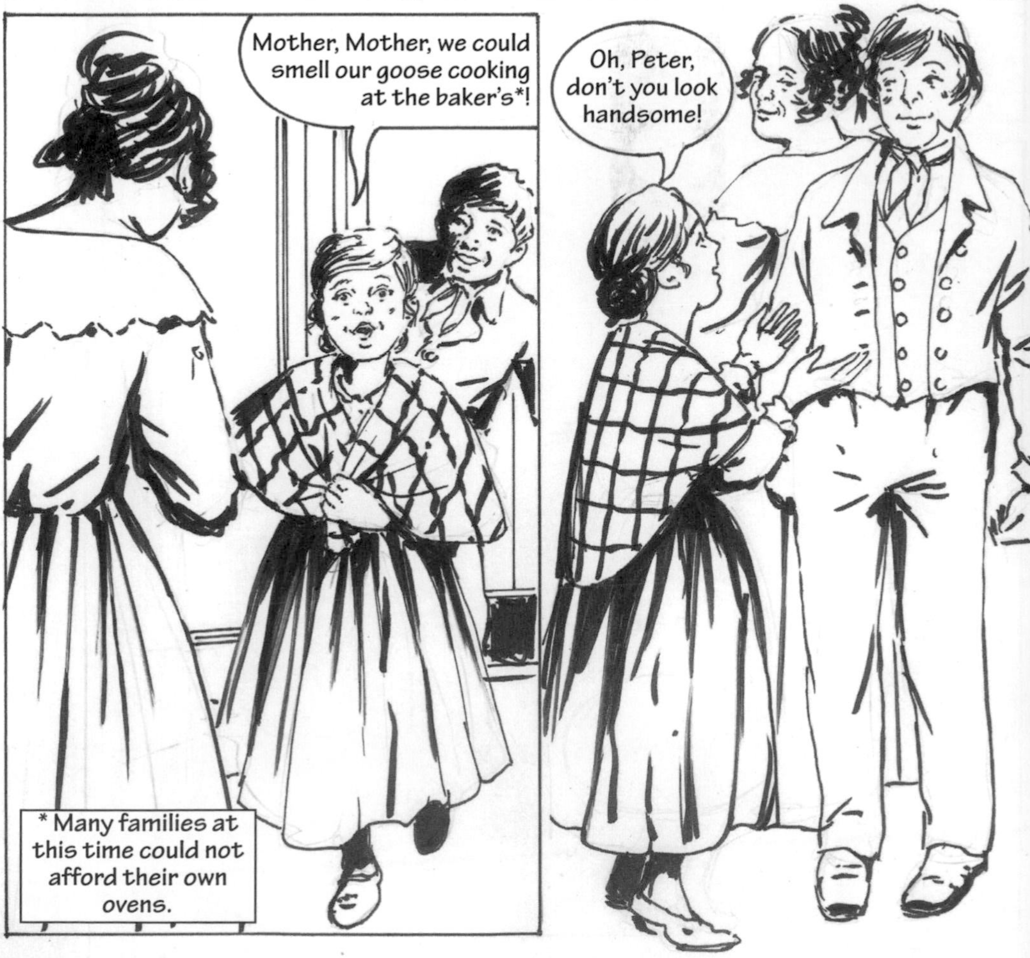
Mother, Mother, we could smell our *goose* cooking at the baker's*!
Oh, Peter, don't you look handsome!
* Many families at this time could not afford their own ovens.

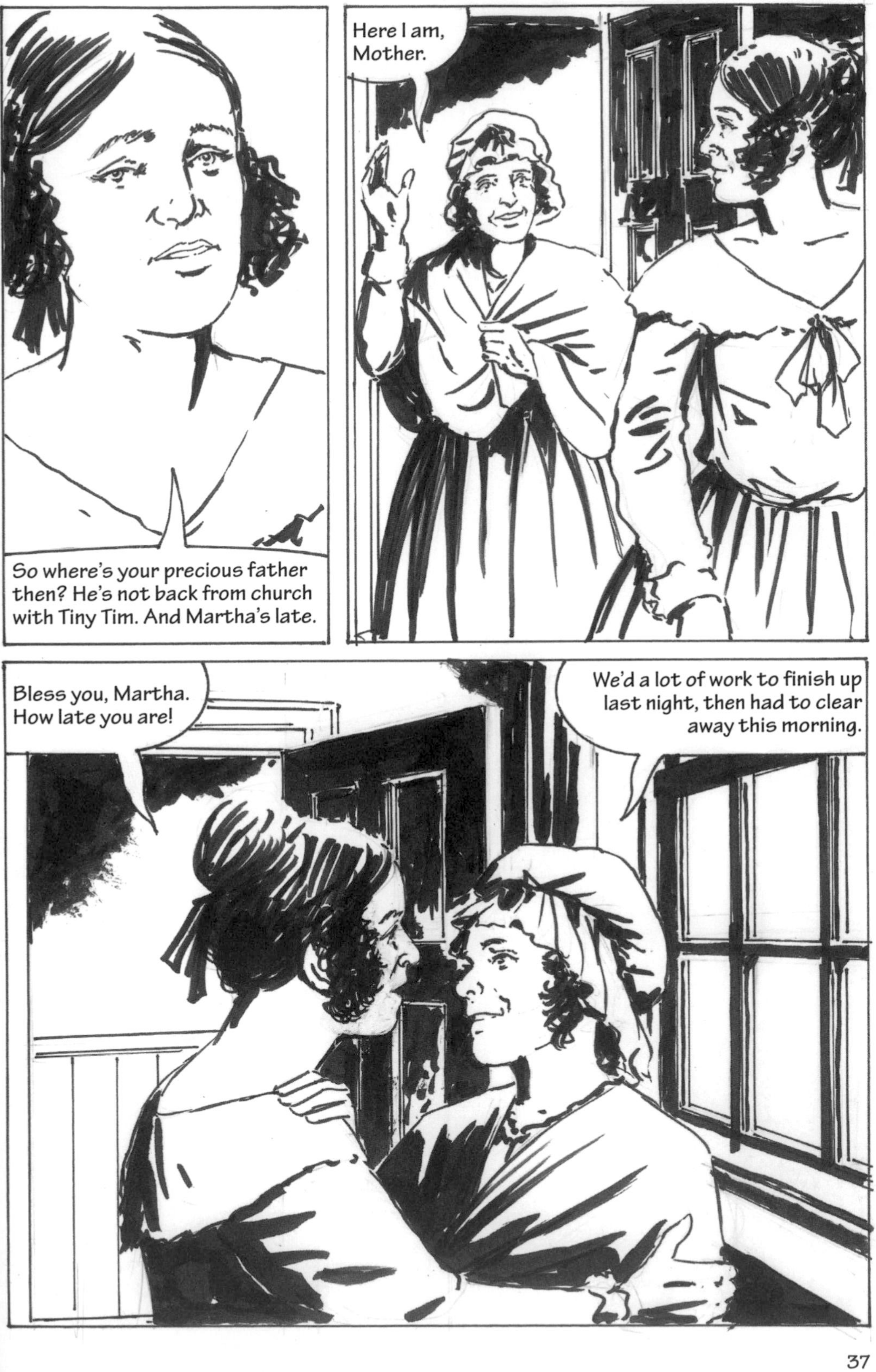
So where's your precious father then? He's not back from church with Tiny Tim. And Martha's late.
Here I am, Mother.
Bless you, Martha. How late you are!
We'd a lot of work to finish up last night, then had to clear away this morning.

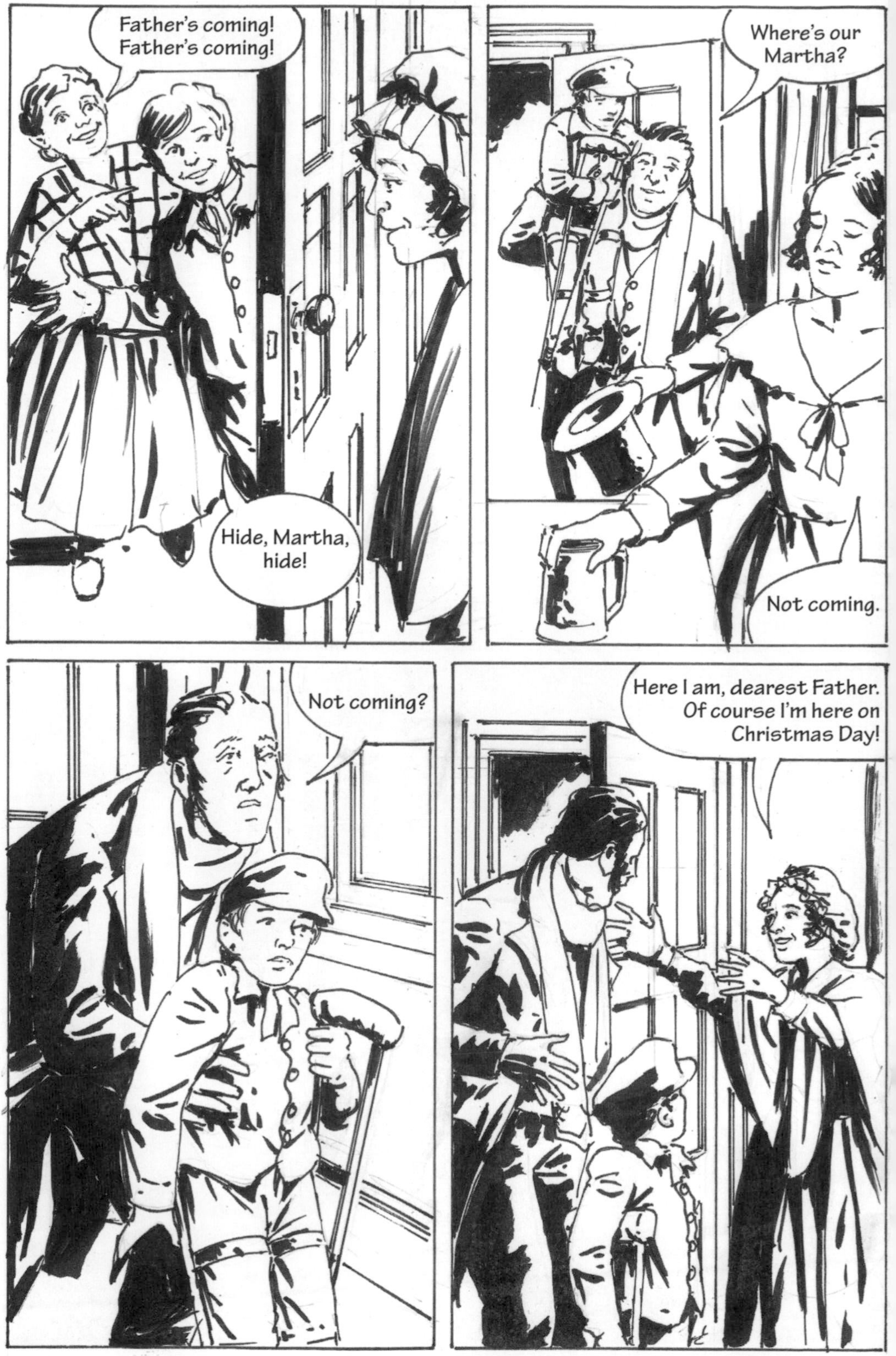
Father's coming!
Father's coming!
Hide, Martha, hide!
Where's our Martha?
Not coming.
Not coming?
Here I am, dearest Father.
Of course I'm here on Christmas Day!

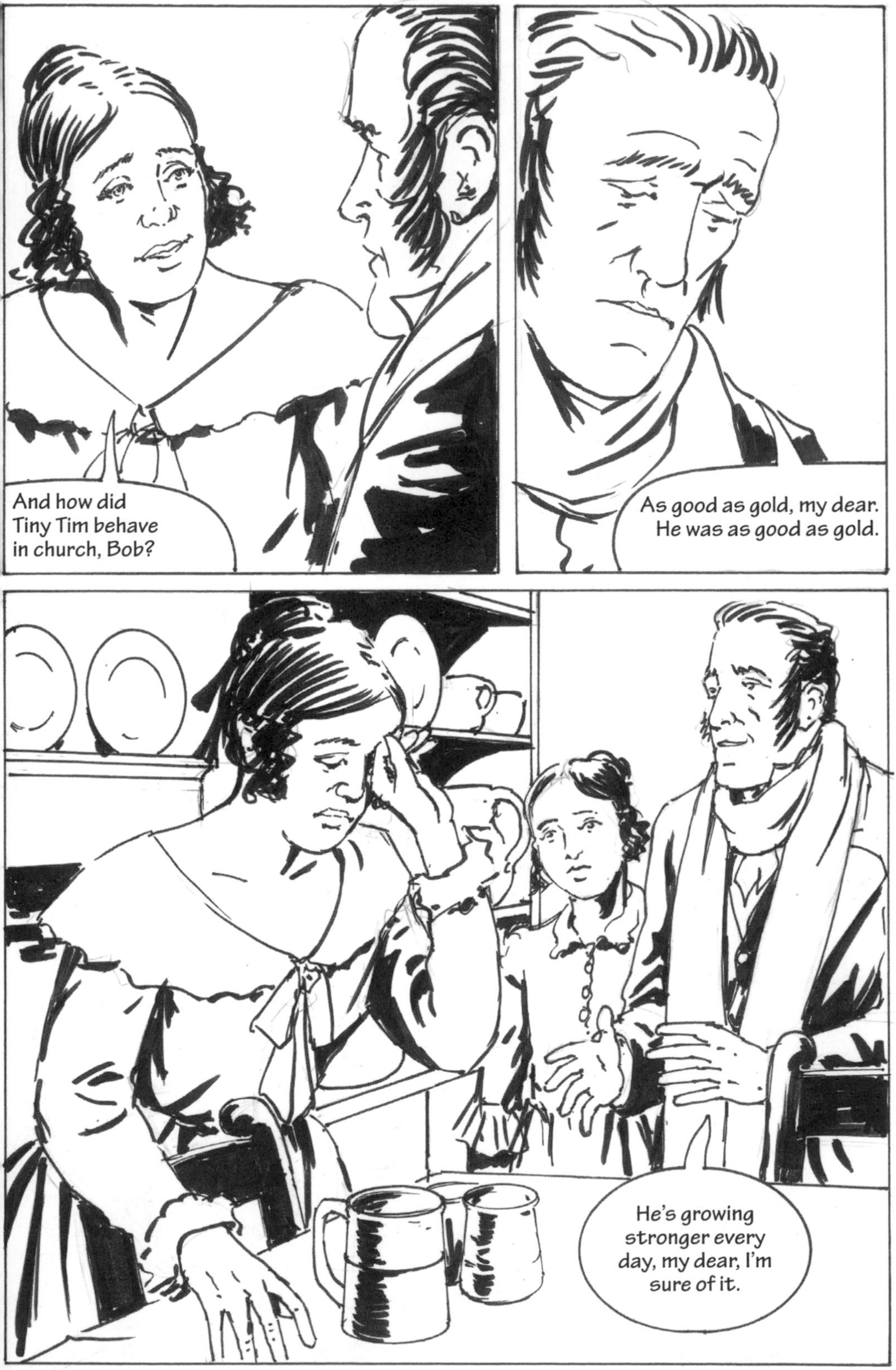
And how did Tiny Tim behave in church, Bob?
As good as gold, my dear. He was as good as gold.
He's growing stronger every day, my dear, I'm sure of it.

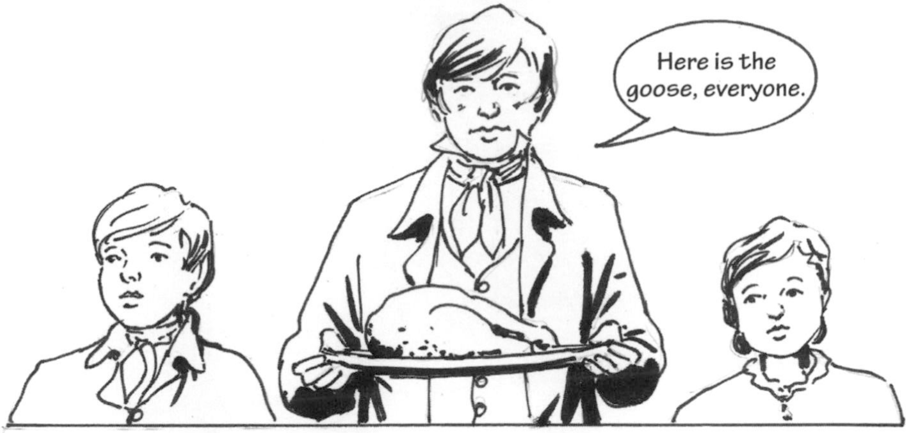
Here is the goose, everyone.

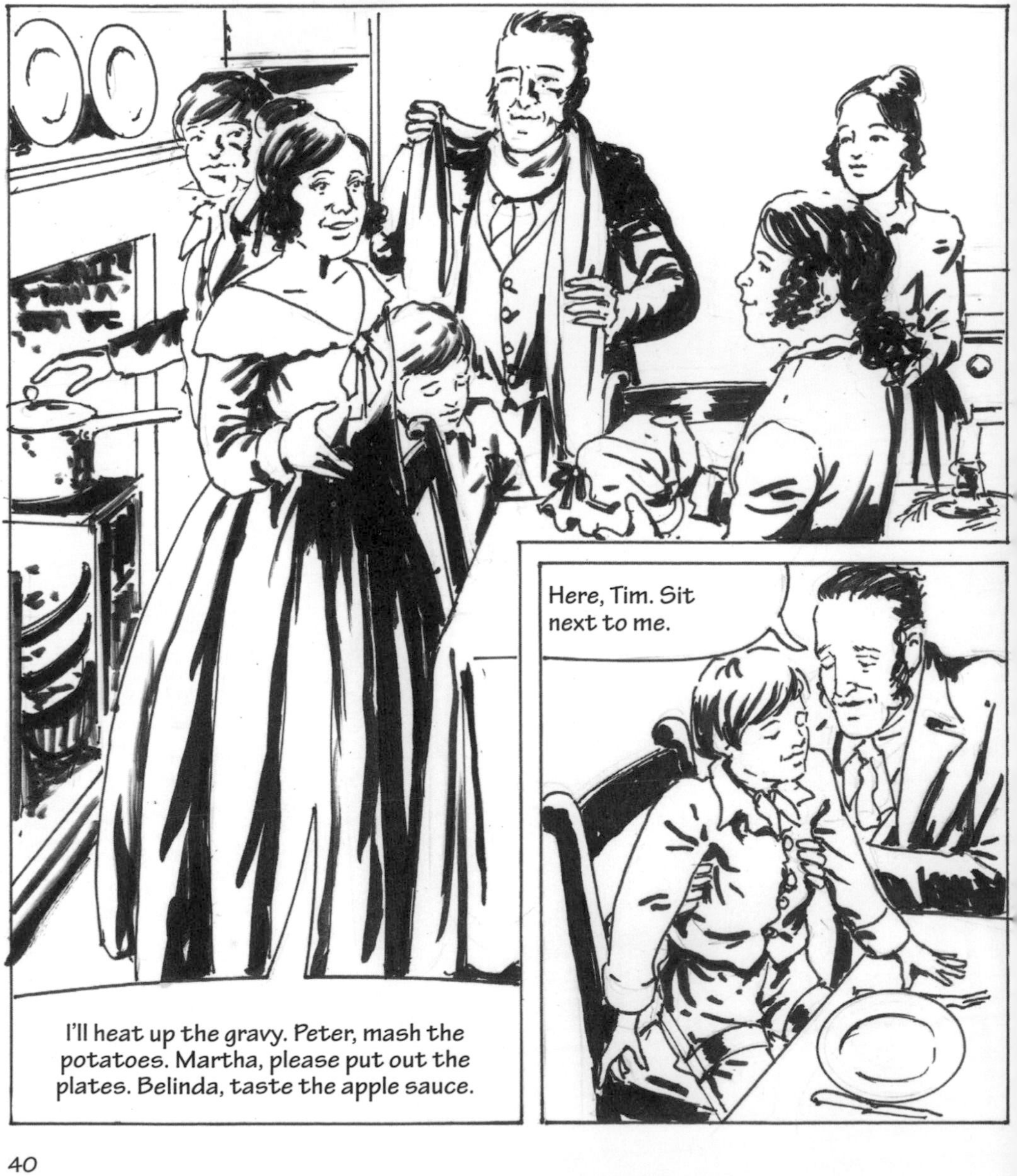
I'll heat up the gravy. Peter, mash the potatoes. Martha, please put out the plates. Belinda, taste the apple sauce.
Here, Tim. Sit next to me.

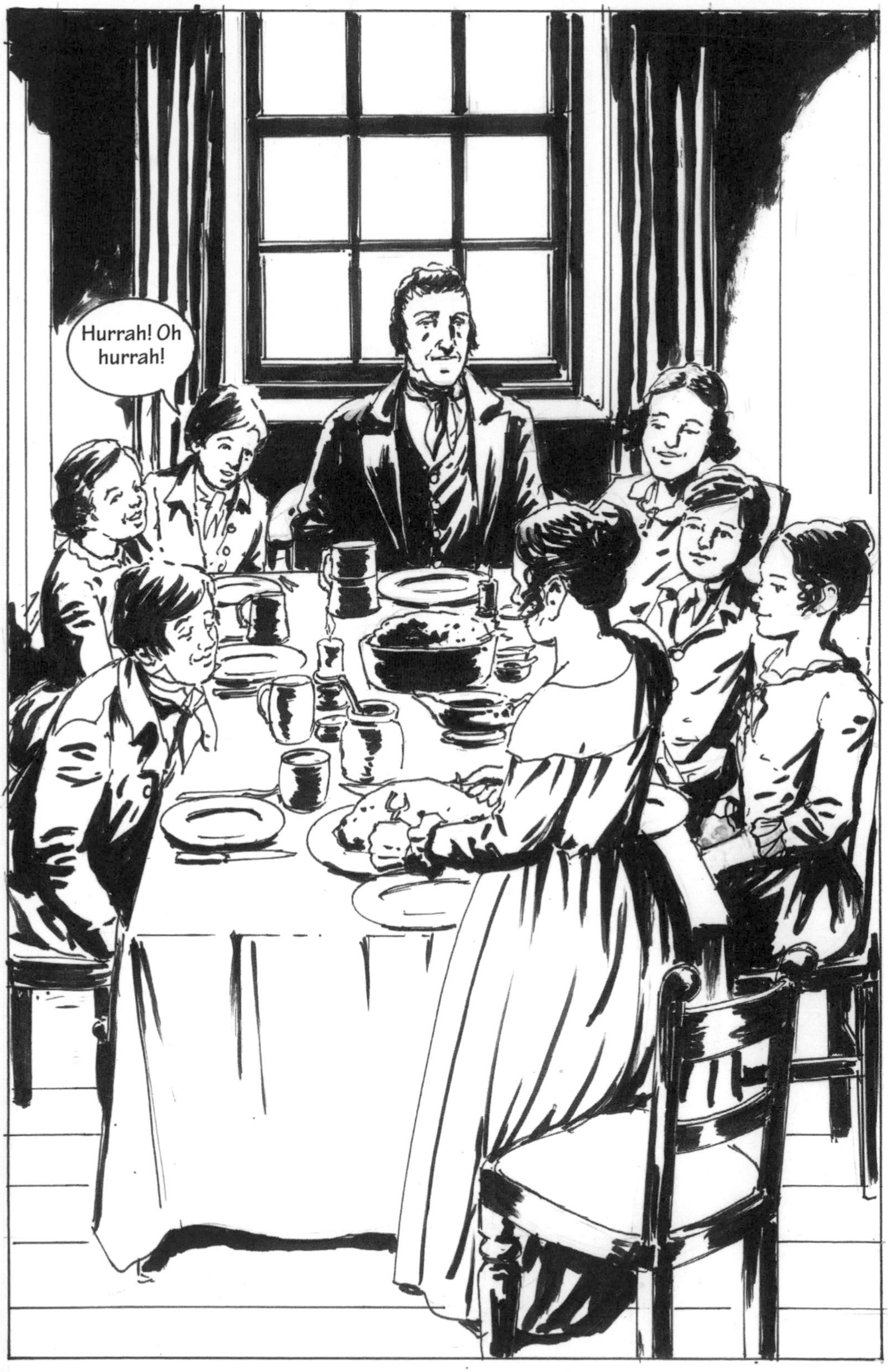
Hurrah! Oh hurrah!

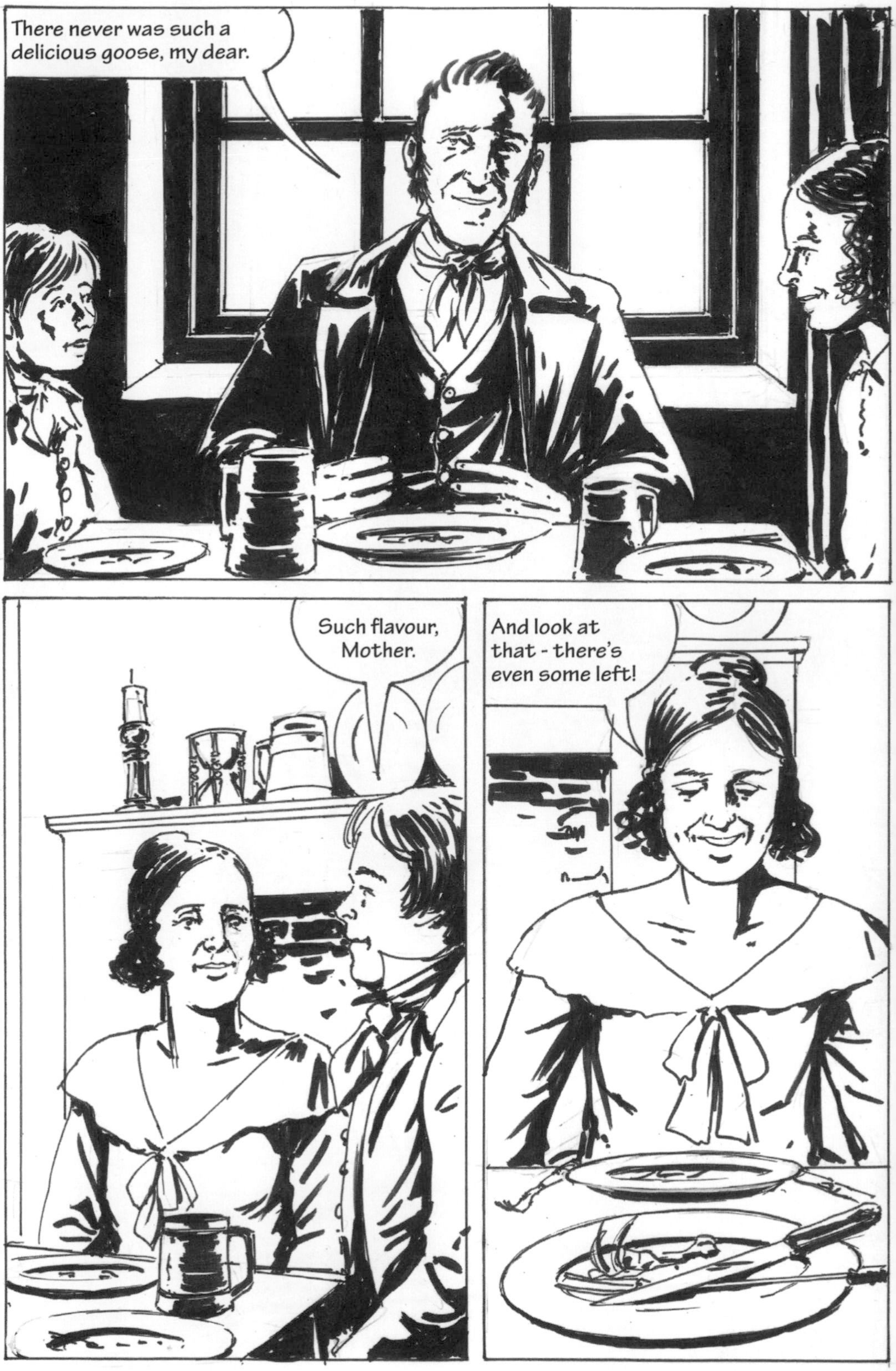
There never was such a delicious goose, my dear.
Such flavour, Mother.
And look at that - there's even some left!

NEXT CAME THE CHRISTMAS PUDDING...

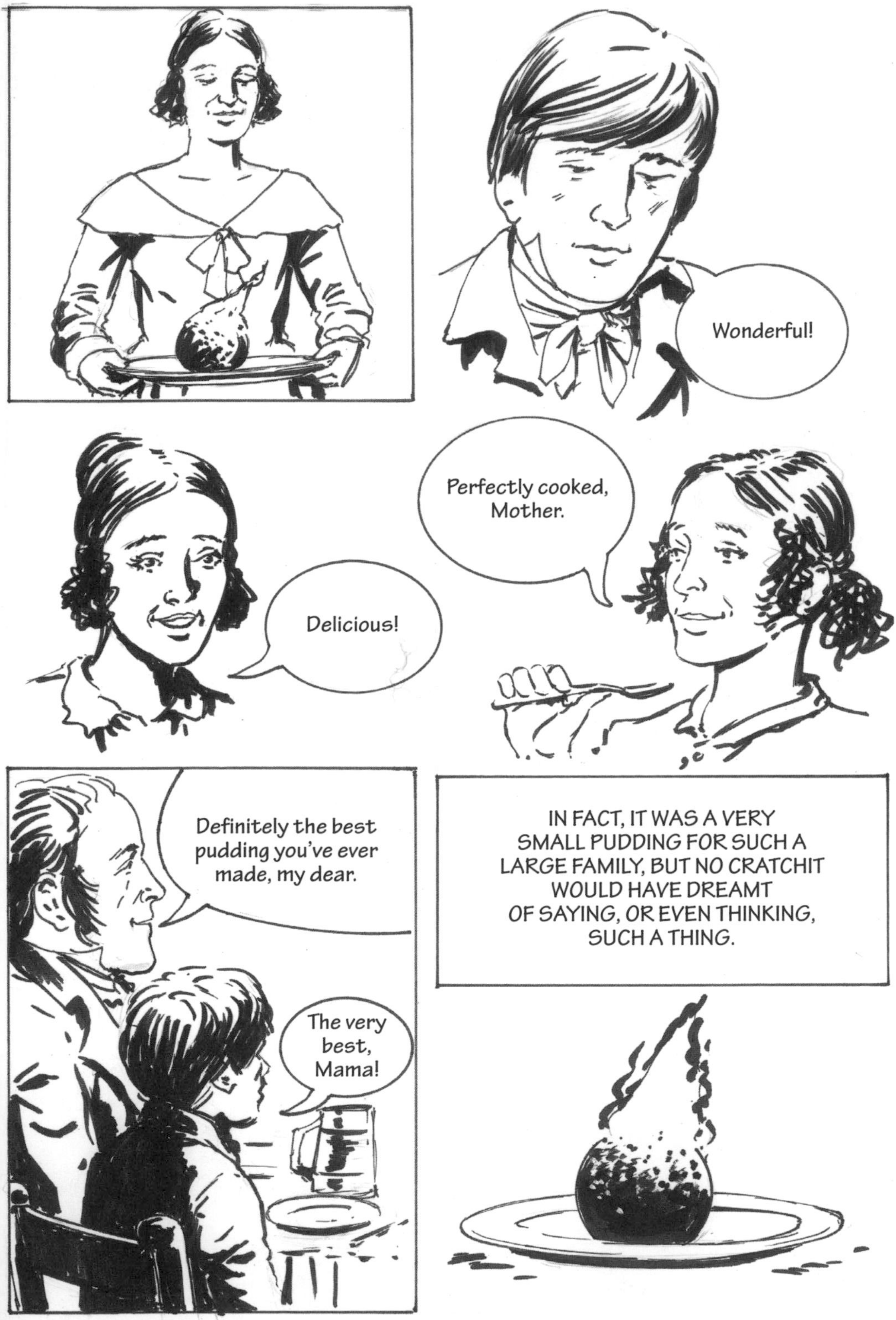

Wonderful!
Perfectly cooked, Mother.
Delicious!
Definitely the best pudding you've ever made, my dear.
The very best, Mama!
IN FACT, IT WAS A VERY SMALL PUDDING FOR SUCH A LARGE FAMILY, BUT NO CRATCHIT WOULD HAVE DREAMT OF SAYING, OR EVEN THINKING, SUCH A THING.

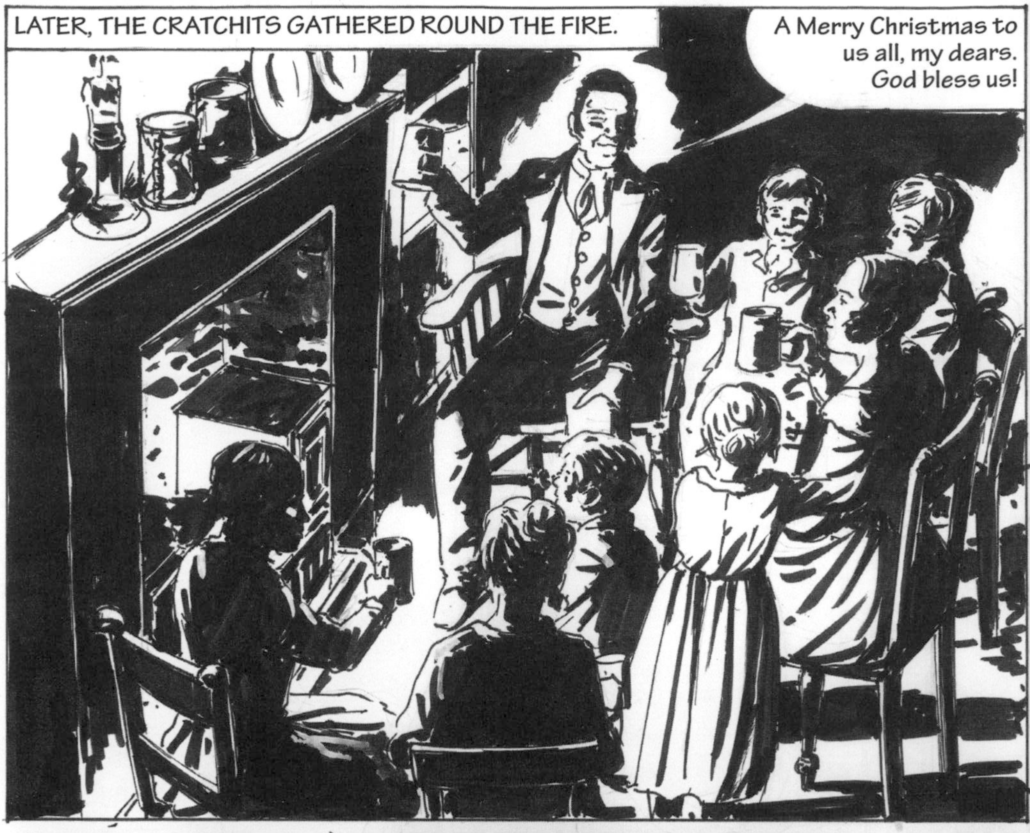
LATER, THE CRATCHITS GATHERED ROUND THE FIRE.
A Merry Christmas to us all, my dears. God bless us!

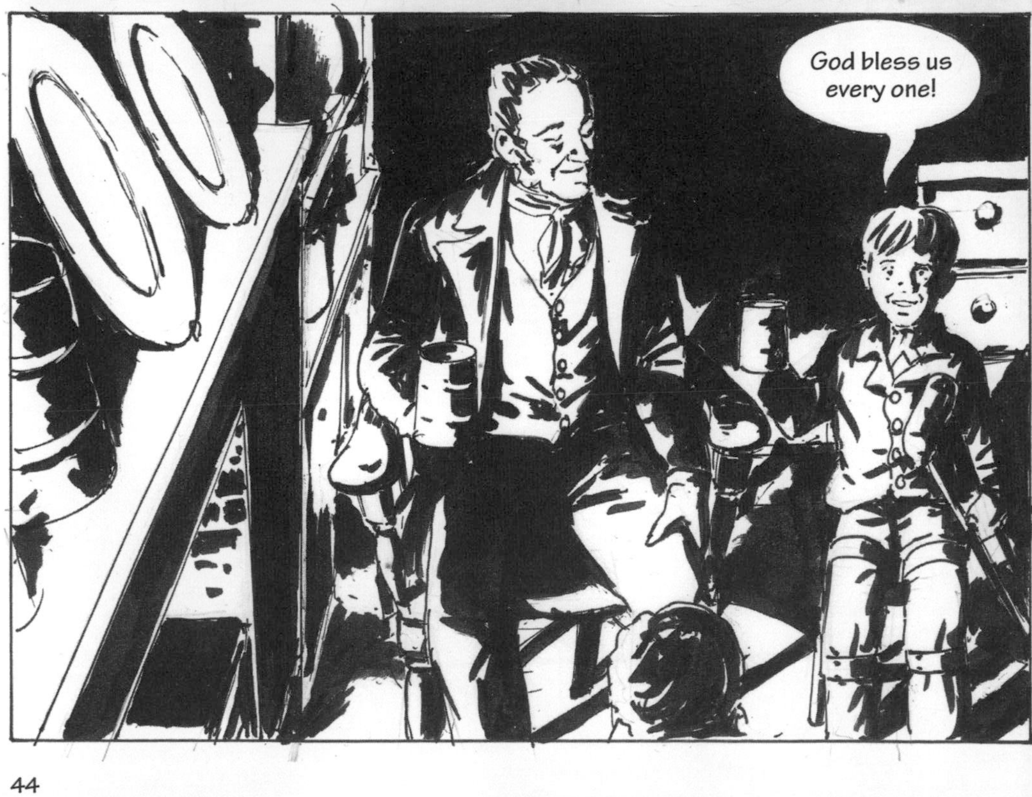
God bless us every one!

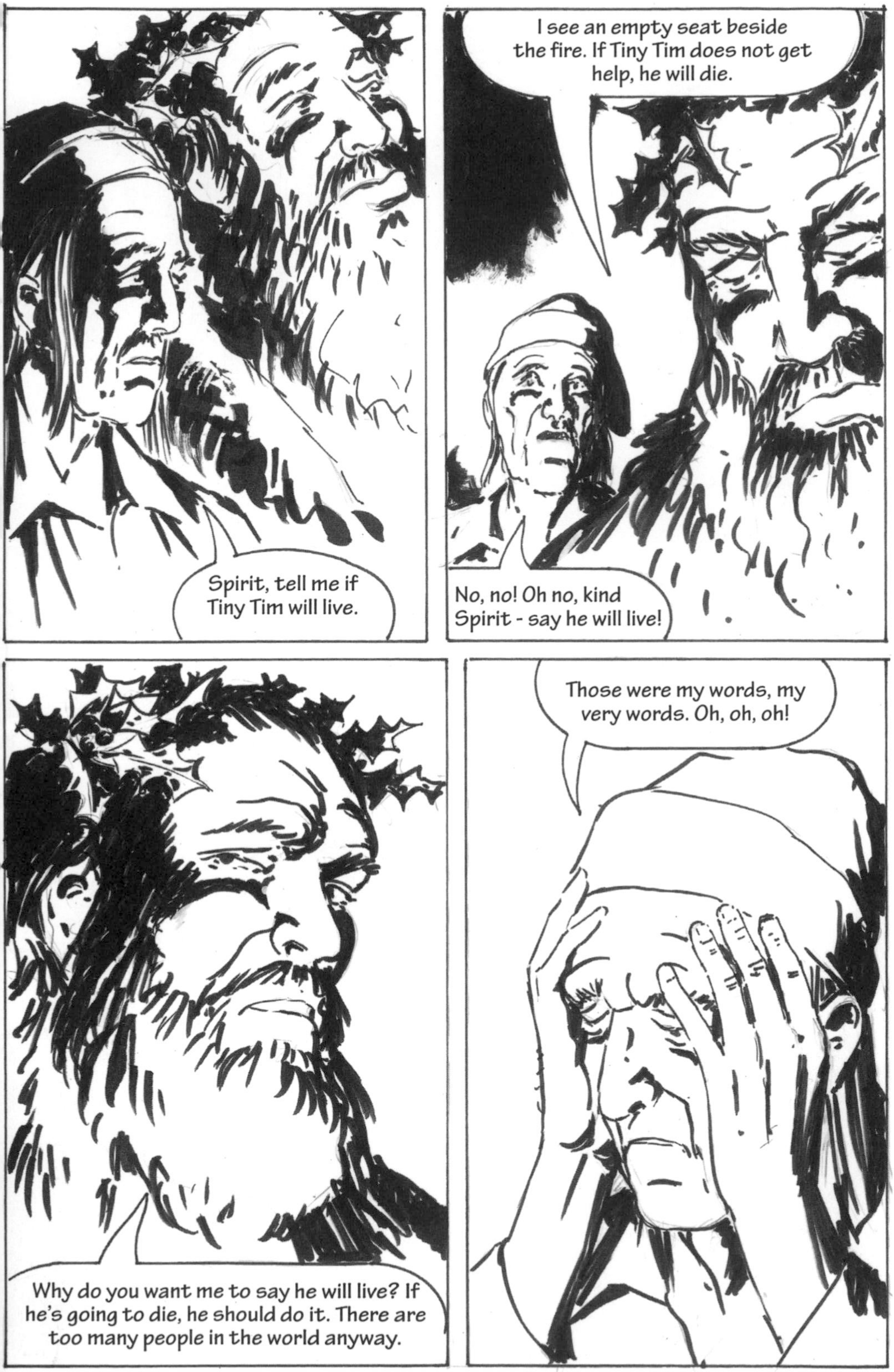
Spirit, tell me if Tiny Tim will live.
I see an empty seat beside the fire. If Tiny Tim does not get help, he will die.
No, no! Oh no, kind Spirit - say he will live!
Why do you want me to say he will live? If he's going to die, he should do it. There are too many people in the world anyway.
Those were my words, my very words. Oh, oh, oh!

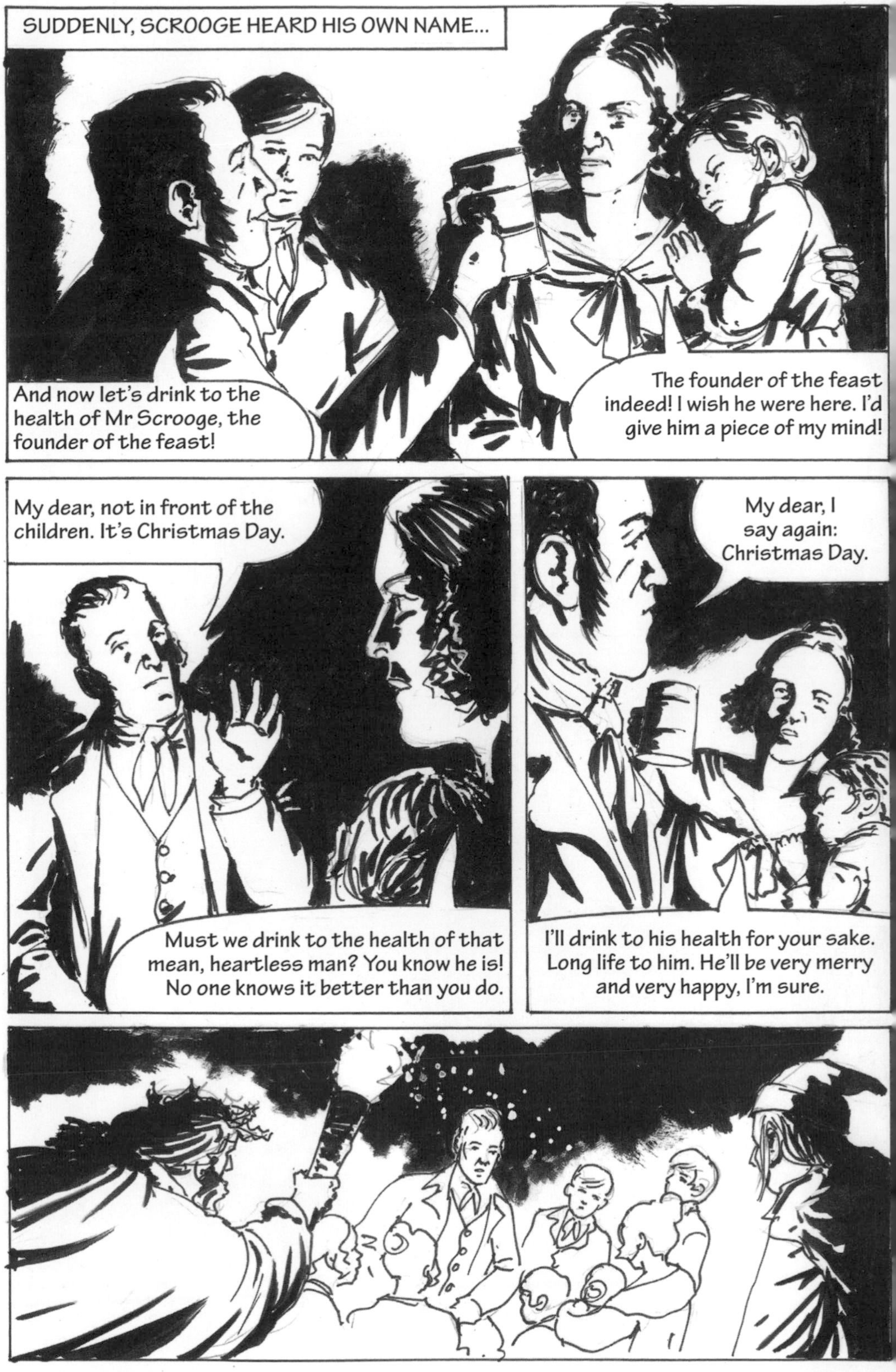
SUDDENLY, SCROOGE HEARD HIS OWN NAME...
And now let's drink to the health of Mr Scrooge, the founder of the feast!
The founder of the feast indeed! I wish he were here. I'd give him a piece of my mind!
My dear, not in front of the children. It's Christmas Day.
Must we drink to the health of that mean, heartless man? You know he is! No one knows it better than you do.
My dear, I say again: Christmas Day.
I'll drink to his health for your sake. Long life to him. He'll be very merry and very happy, I'm sure.

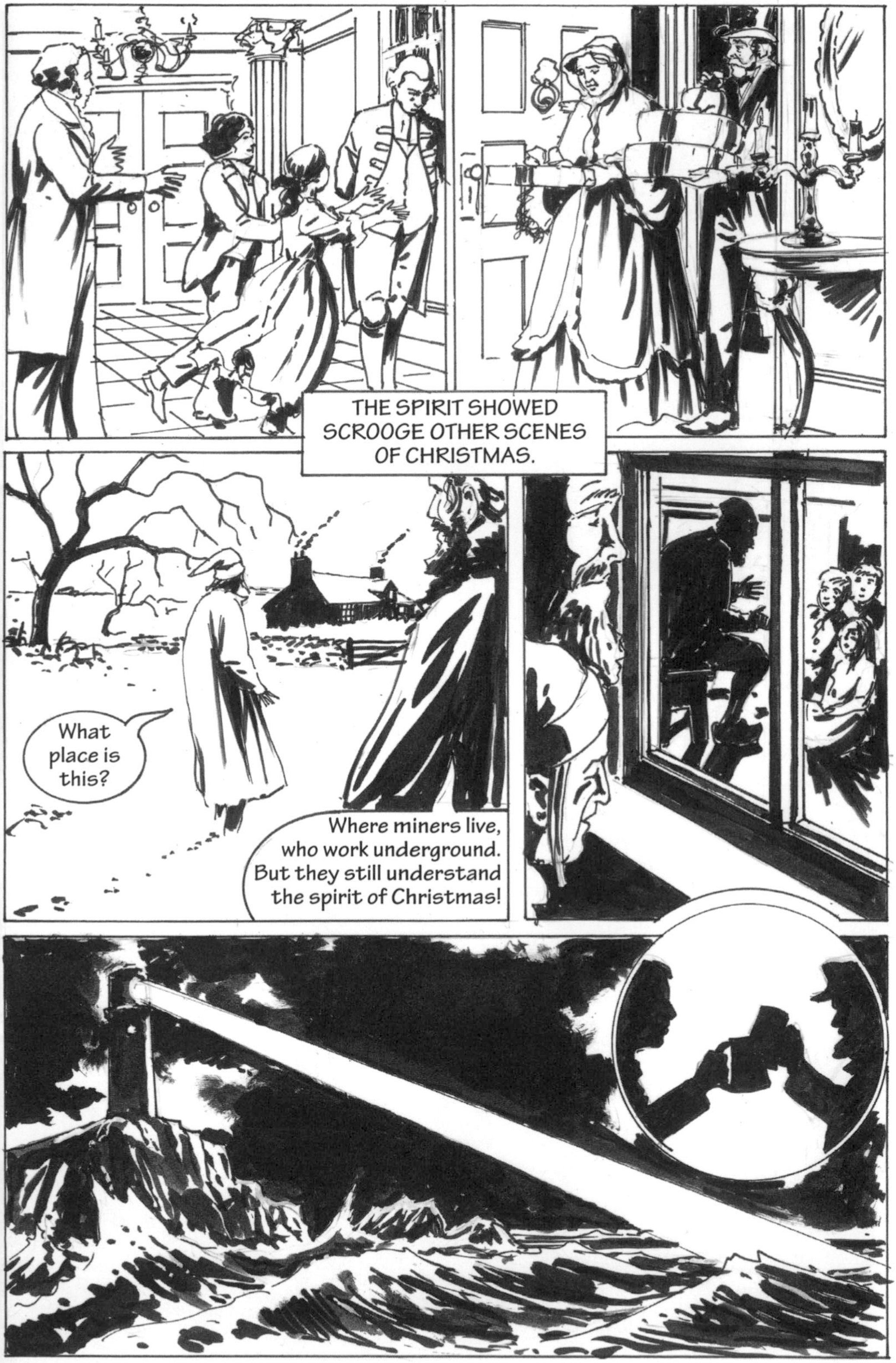
THE SPIRIT SHOWED SCROOGE OTHER SCENES OF CHRISTMAS.
What place is this?
Where miners live, who work underground. But they still understand the spirit of Christmas!

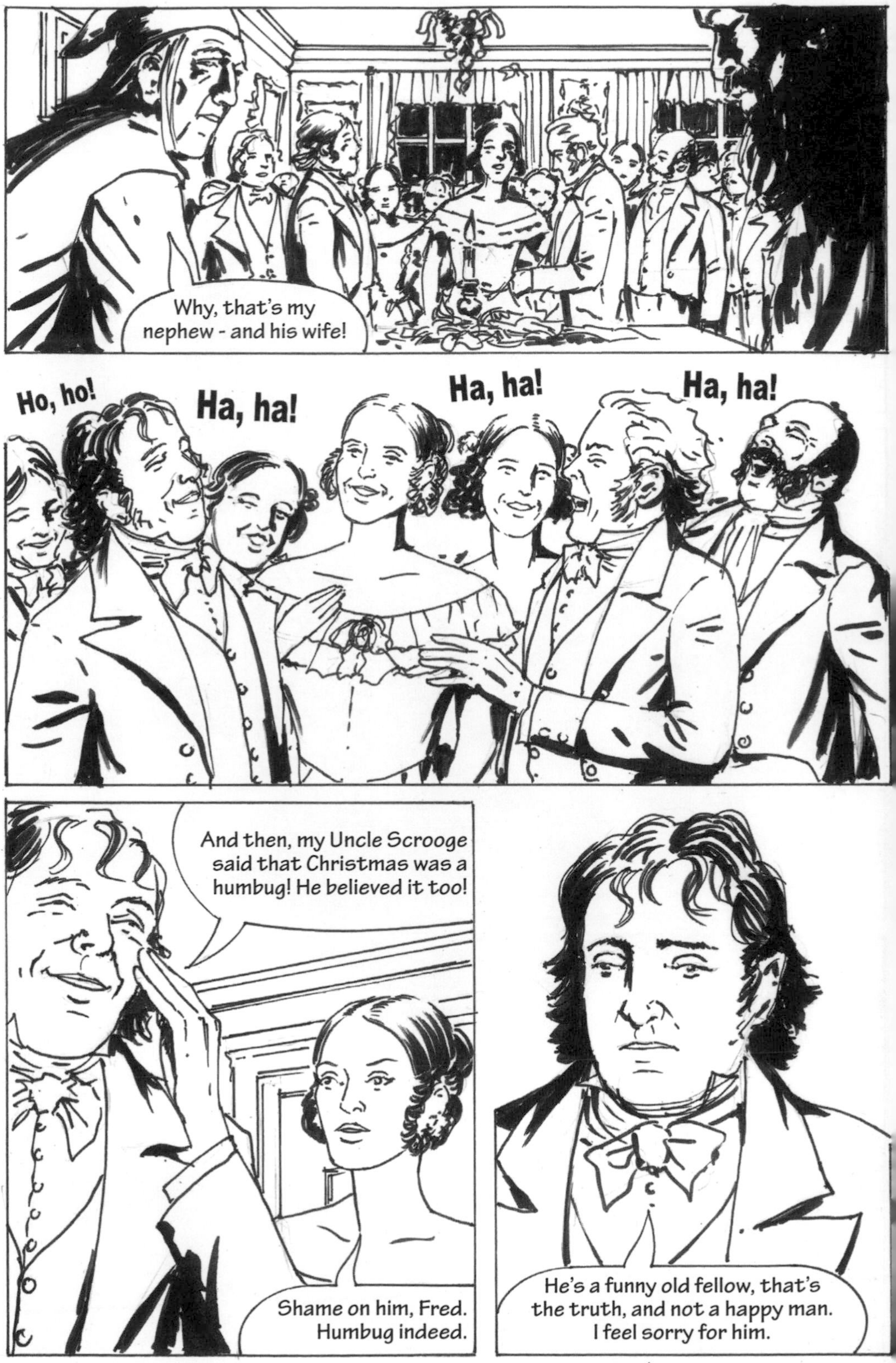
Why, that's my nephew - and his wife!
Ho, ho!
Ha, ha!
Ha, ha!
Ha, ha!
And then, my Uncle Scrooge said that Christmas was a humbug! He believed it too!
Shame on him, Fred. Humbug indeed.
He's a funny old fellow, that's the truth, and not a happy man. I feel sorry for him.

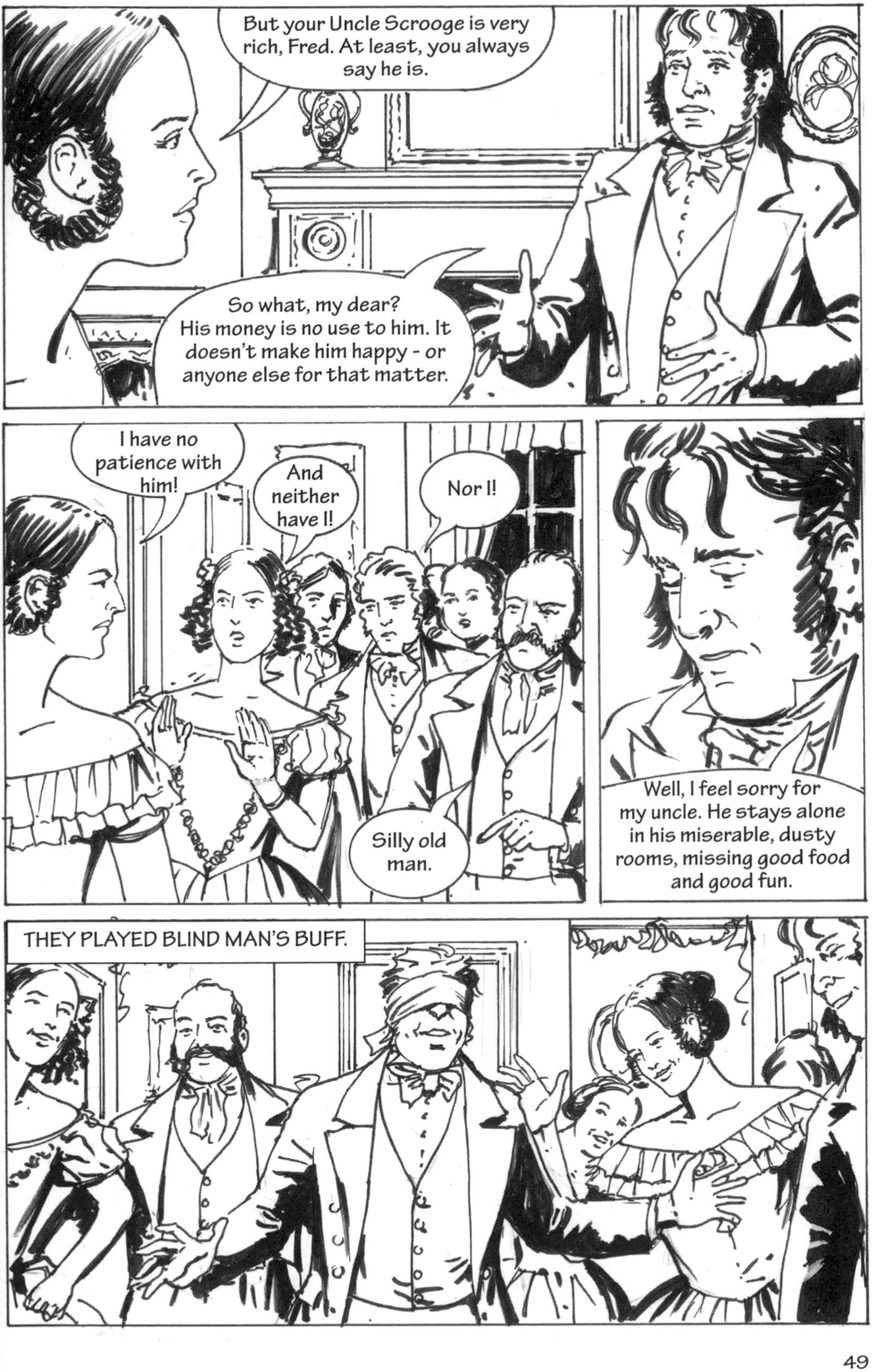

But your Uncle Scrooge is very rich, Fred. At least, you always say he is.
So what, my dear? His money is no use to him. It doesn't make him happy - or anyone else for that matter.
I have no patience with him!
And neither have I!
Nor I!
Silly old man.
Well, I feel sorry for my uncle. He stays alone in his miserable, dusty rooms, missing good food and good fun.
THEY PLAYED BLIND MAN'S BUFF.

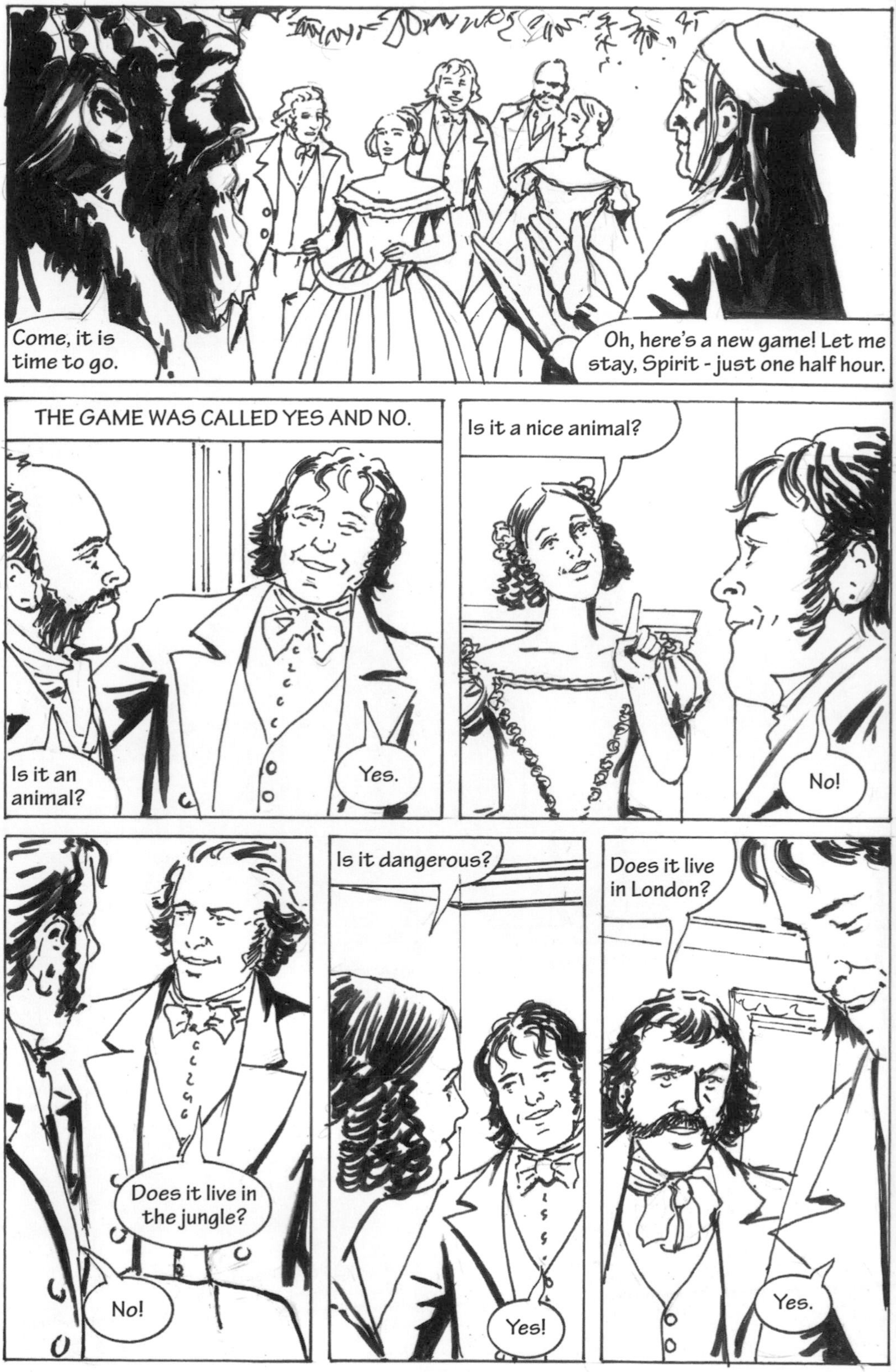
Come, it is time to go.
Oh, here's a new game! Let me stay, Spirit - just one half hour.
THE GAME WAS CALLED YES AND NO.
Is it an animal?
Yes.
Is it a nice animal?
No!
Does it live in the jungle?
No!
Is it dangerous?
Yes!
Does it live in London?
Yes.

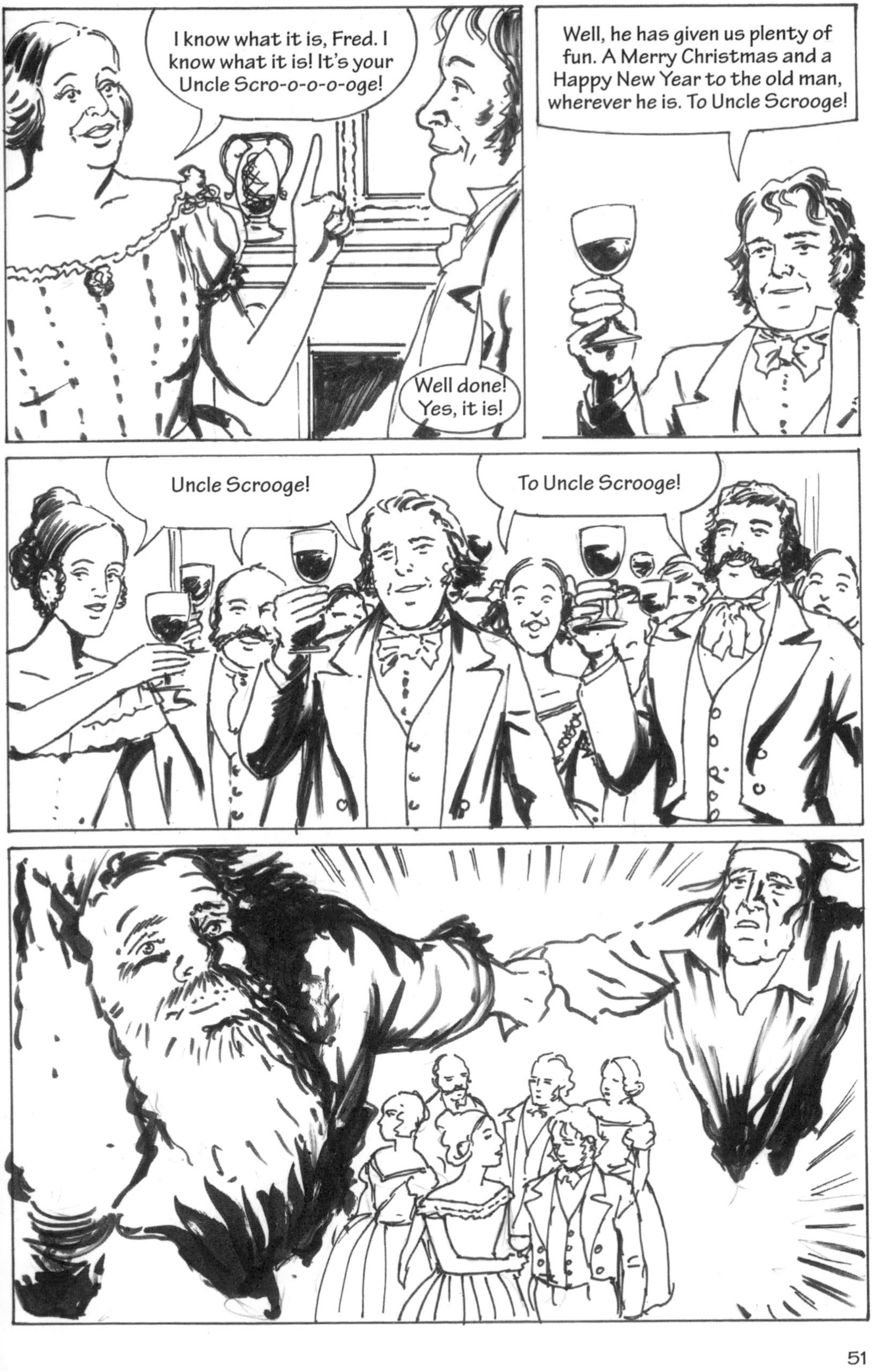
I know what it is, Fred. I know what it is! It's your Uncle Scro-o-o-o-oge!
Well done! Yes, it is!
Well, he has given us plenty of fun. A Merry Christmas and a Happy New Year to the old man, wherever he is. To Uncle Scrooge!
Uncle Scrooge!
To Uncle Scrooge!

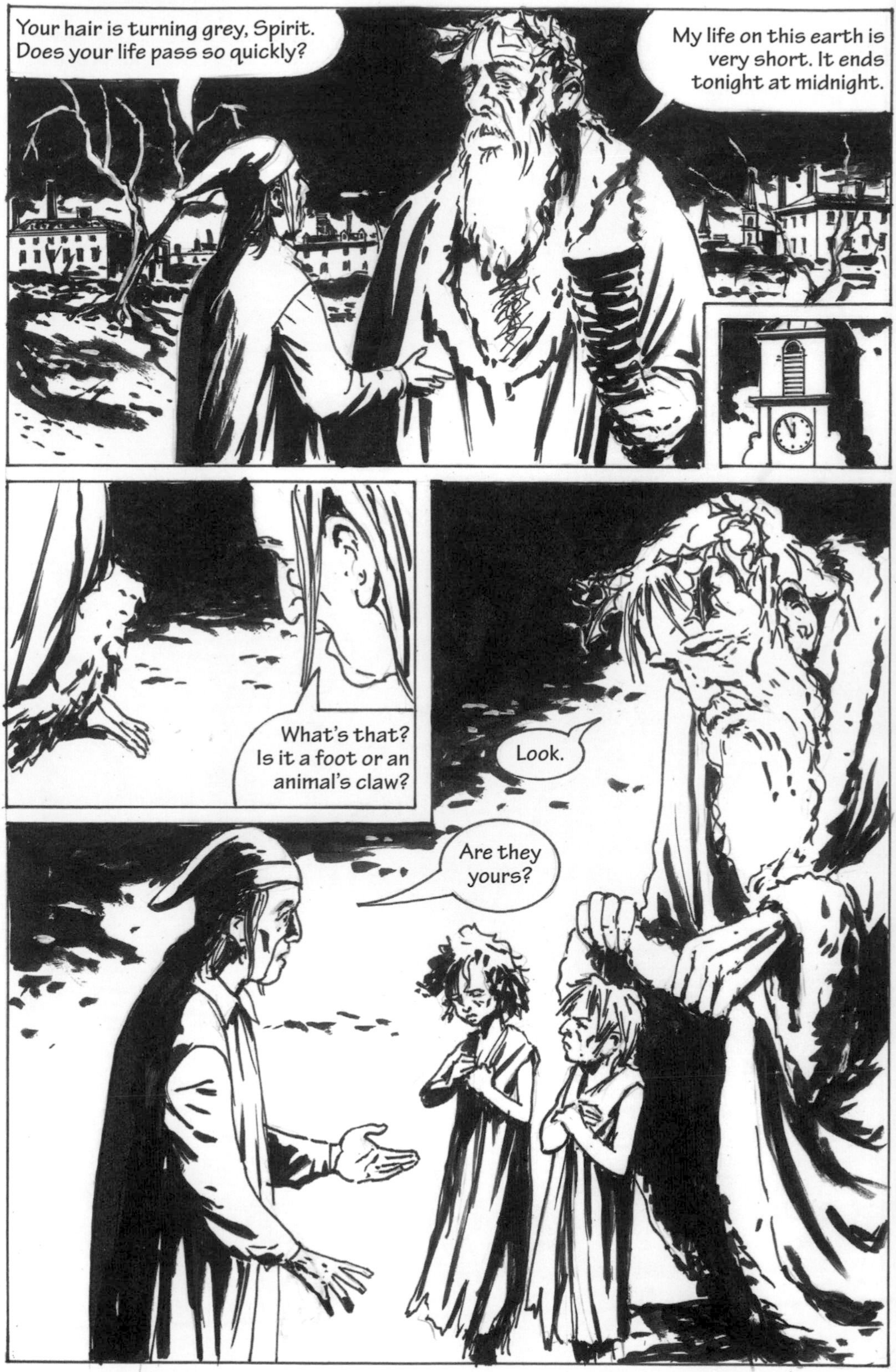
Your hair is turning grey, Spirit. Does your life pass so quickly?
My life on this earth is very short. It ends tonight at midnight.
What's that? Is it a foot or an animal's claw?
Look.
Are they yours?

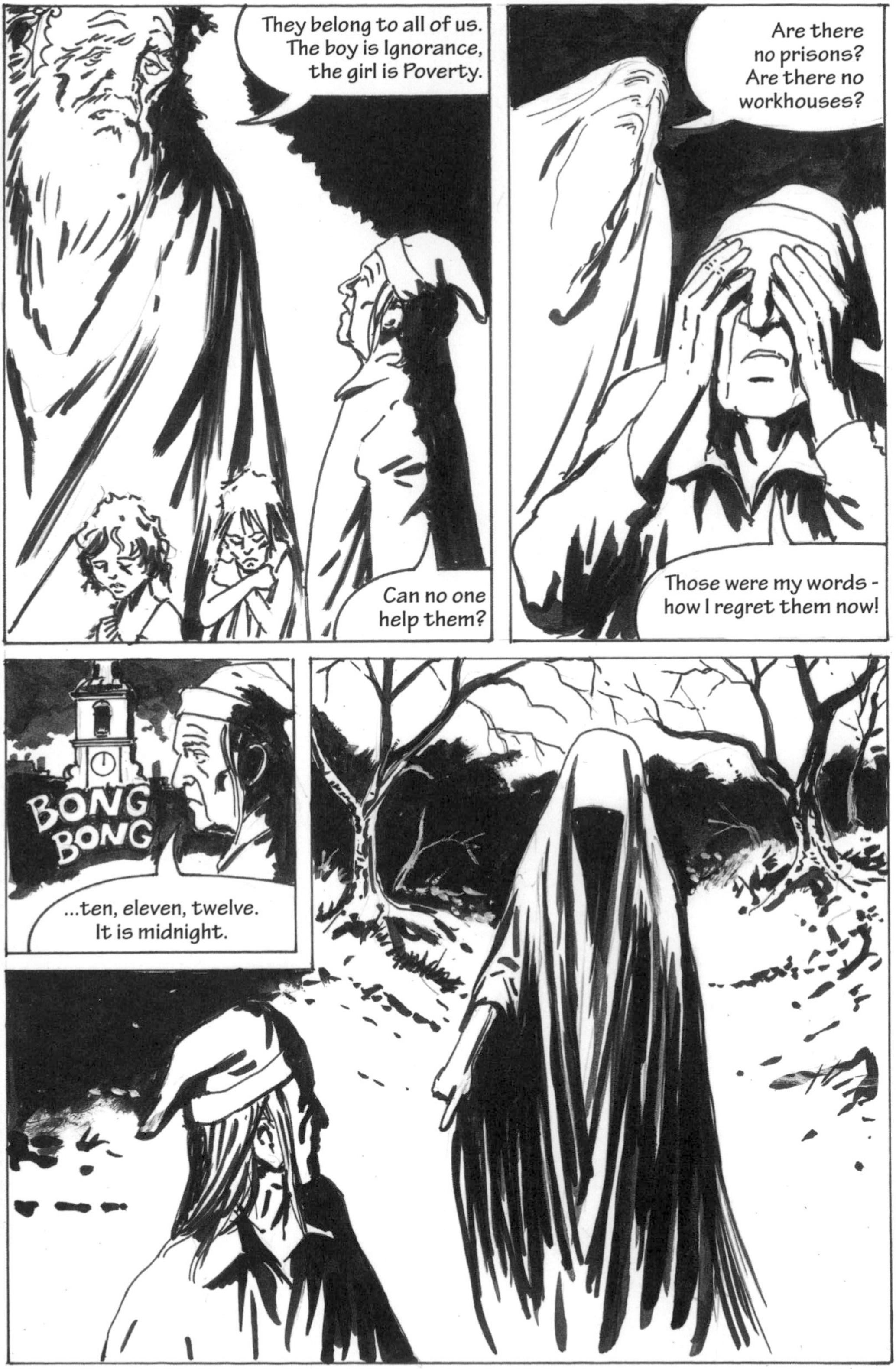
They belong to all of us. The boy is Ignorance, the girl is Poverty.
Can no one help them?
Are there no prisons? Are there no workhouses?
Those were my words - how I regret them now!
BONG BONG
...ten, eleven, twelve. It is midnight.

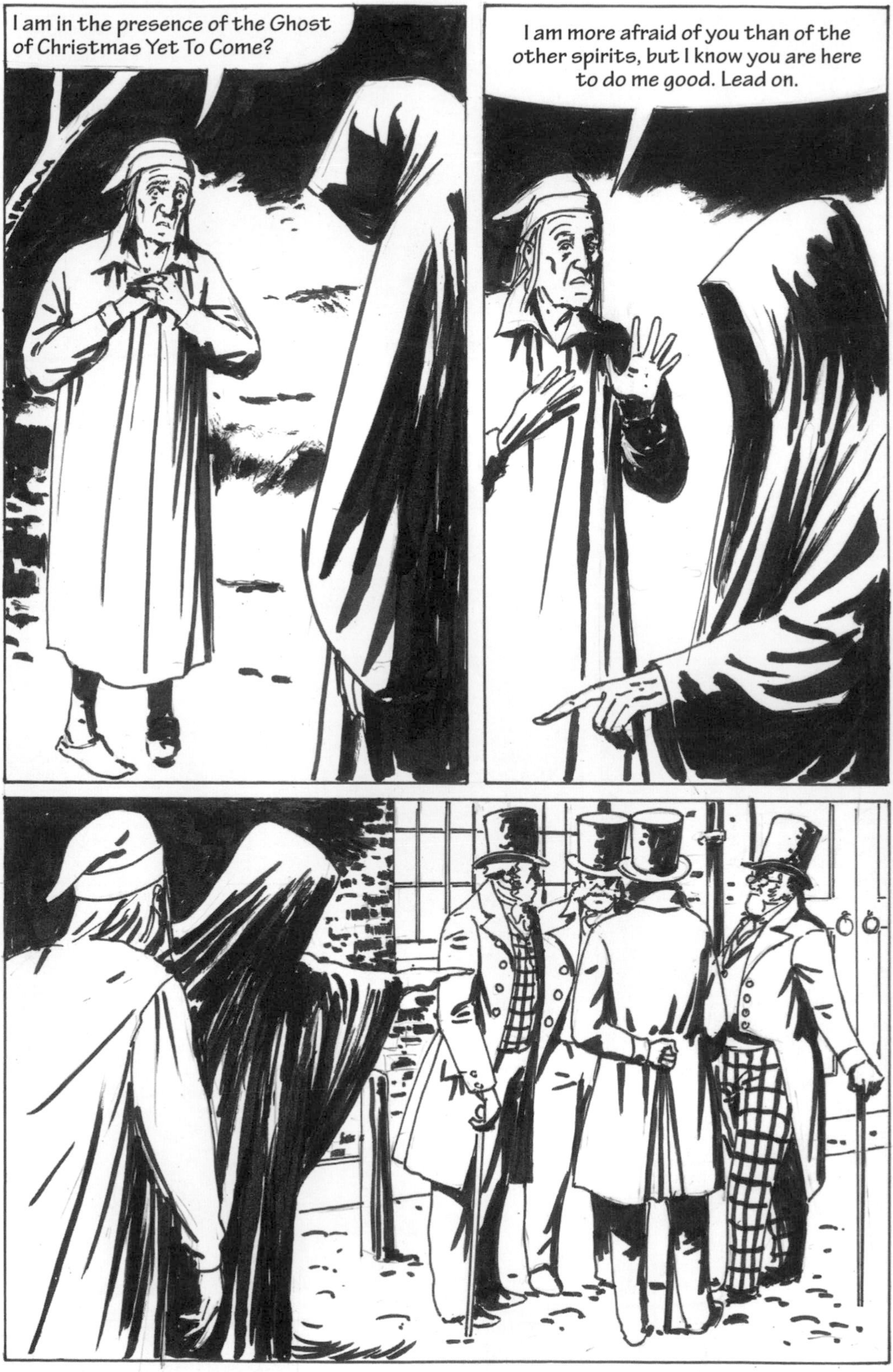
I am in the presence of the Ghost of Christmas Yet To Come?
I am more afraid of you than of the other spirits, but I know you are here to do me good. Lead on.

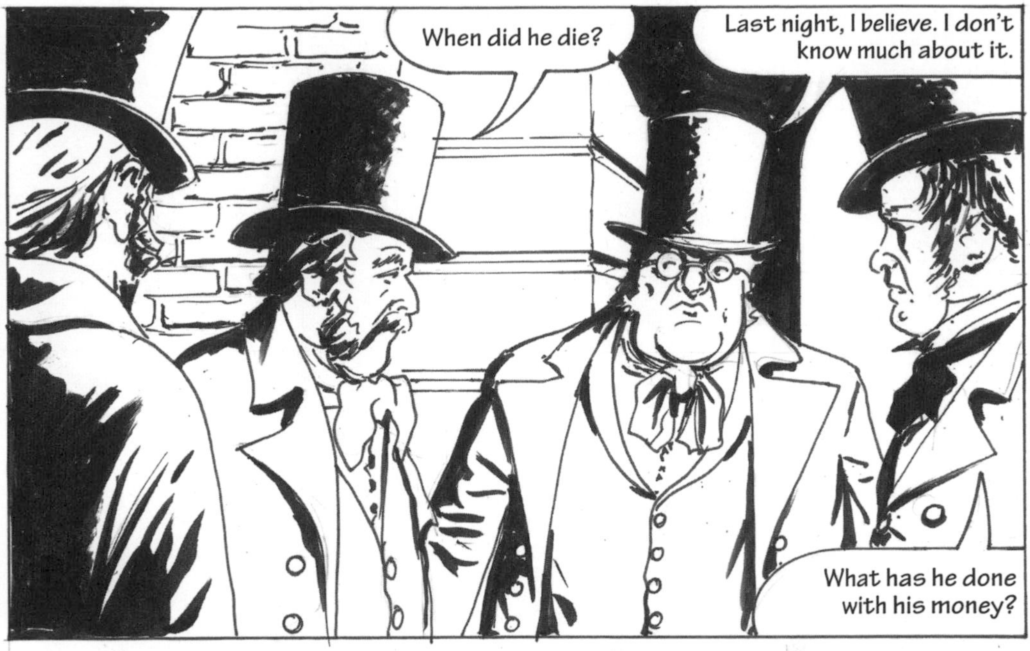
When did he die?
Last night, I believe. I don't know much about it.
What has he done with his money?

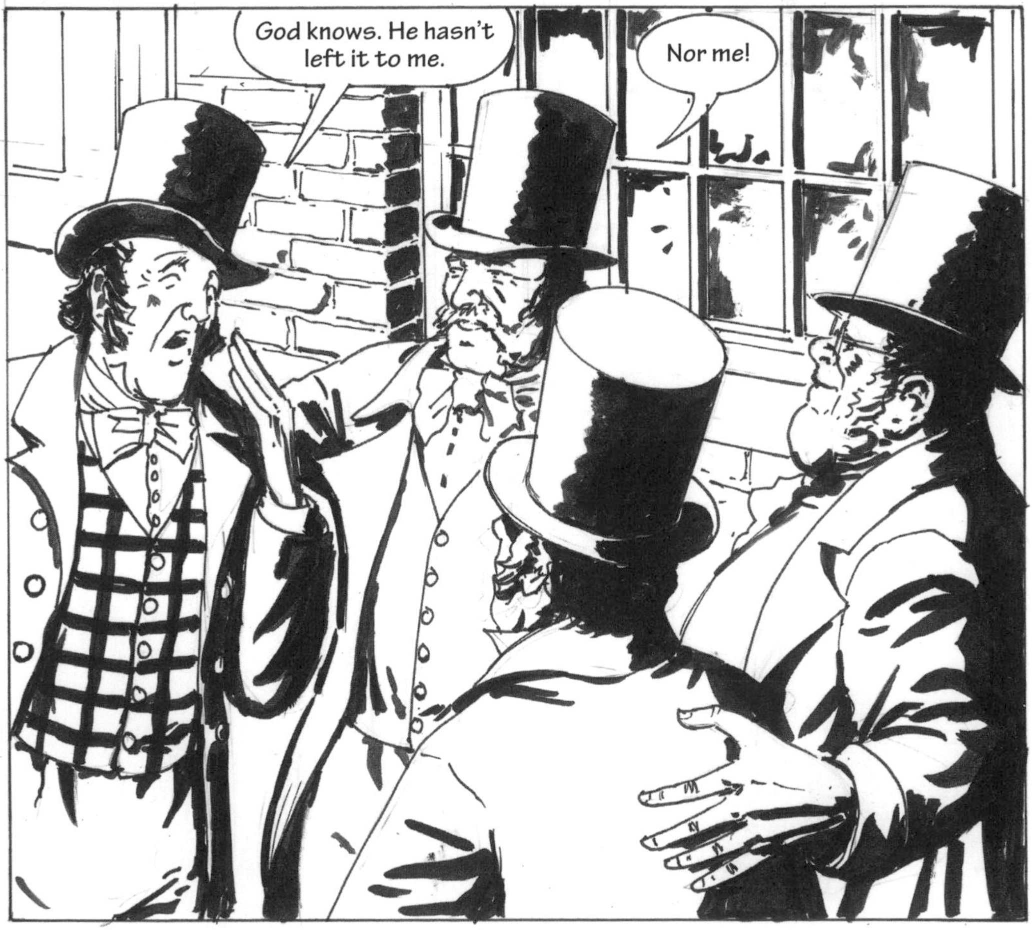
God knows. He hasn't left it to me.
Nor me!

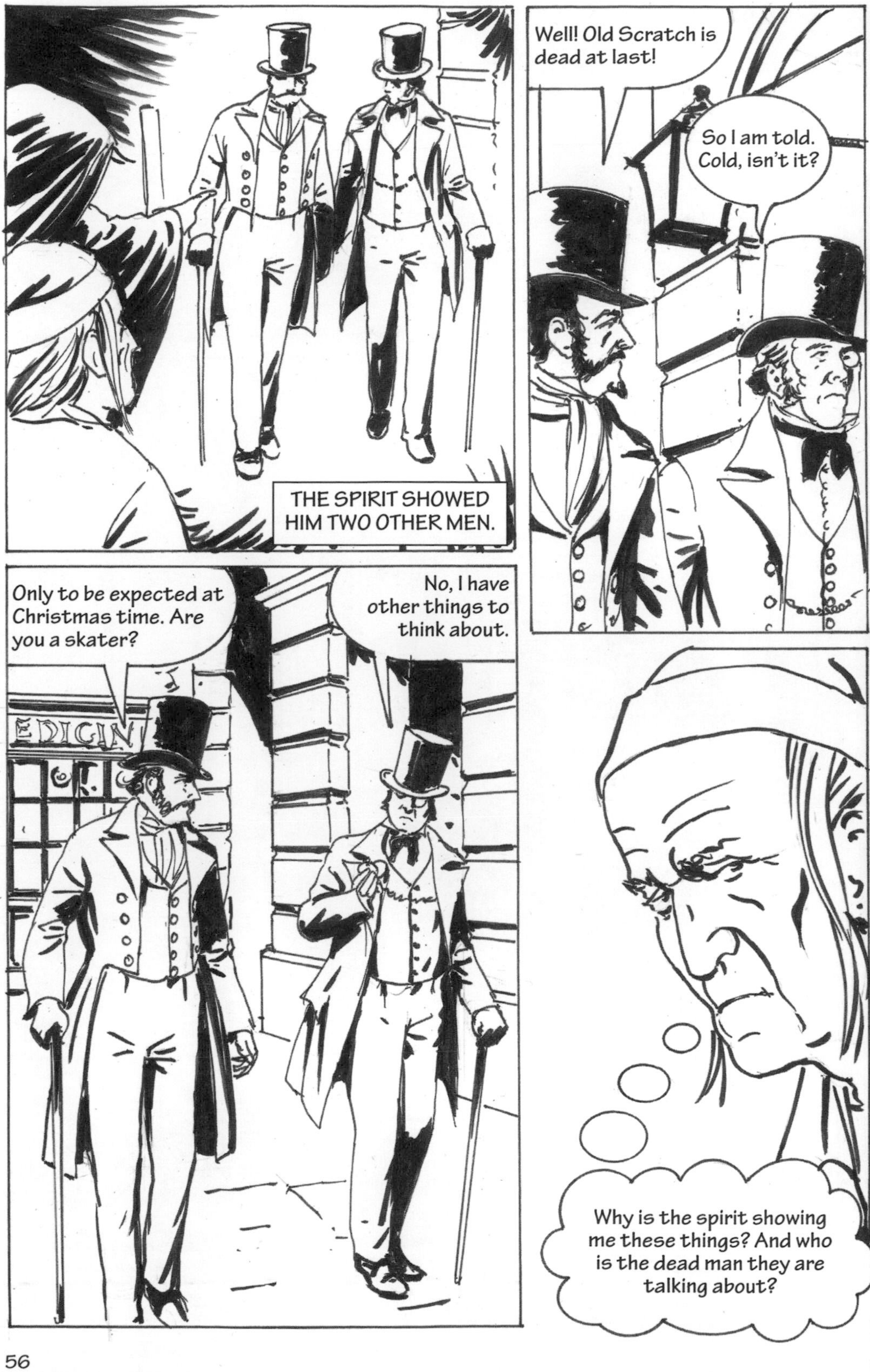
THE SPIRIT SHOWED HIM TWO OTHER MEN.
Well! Old Scratch is dead at last!
So I am told. Cold, isn't it?
Only to be expected at Christmas time. Are you a skater?
No, I have other things to think about.
Why is the spirit showing me these things? And who is the dead man they are talking about?

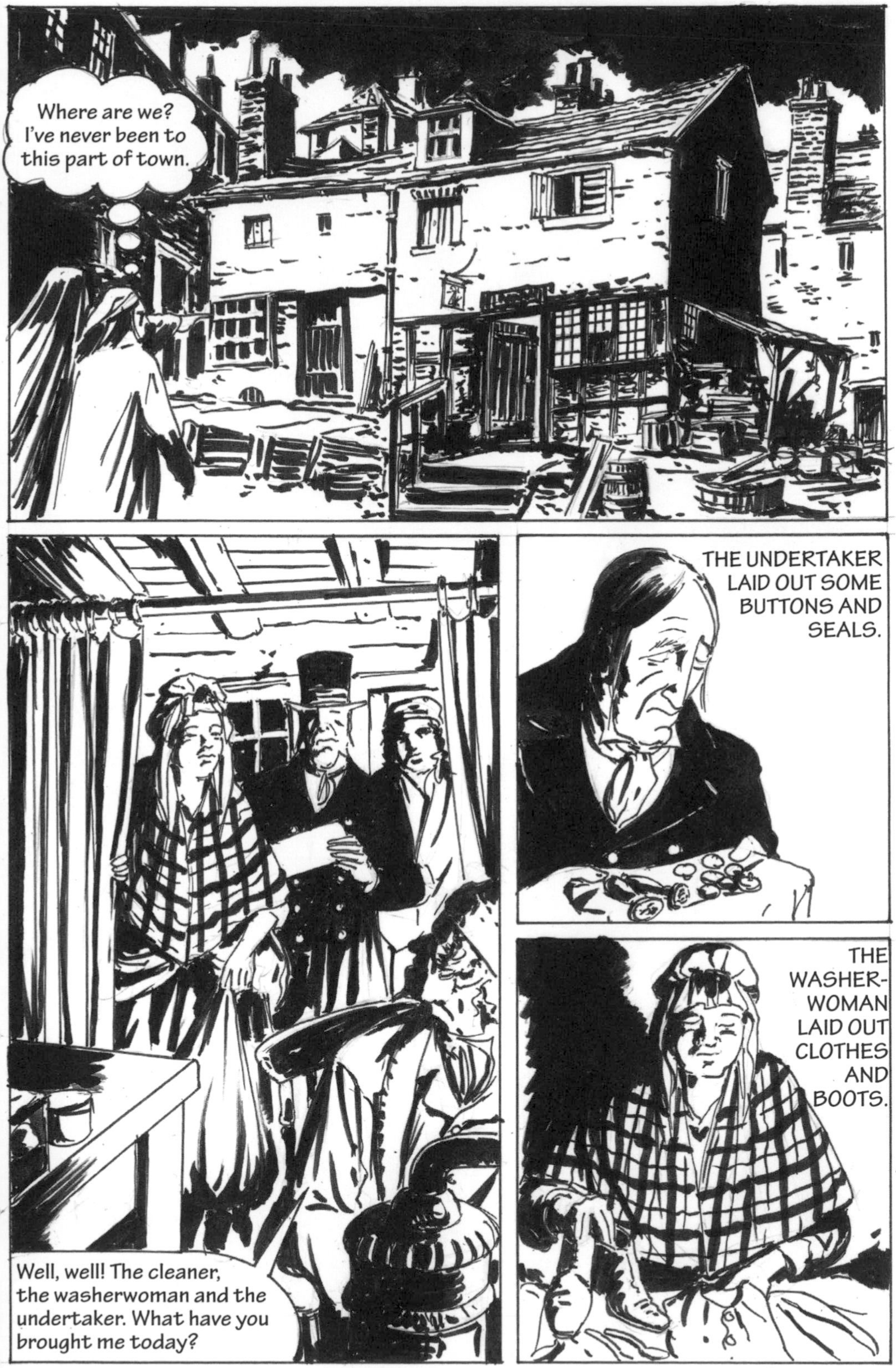
Where are we? I've never been to this part of town.
Well, well! The cleaner, the washerwoman and the undertaker. What have you brought me today?
THE UNDERTAKER LAID OUT SOME BUTTONS AND SEALS.
THE WASHER-WOMAN LAID OUT CLOTHES AND BOOTS.

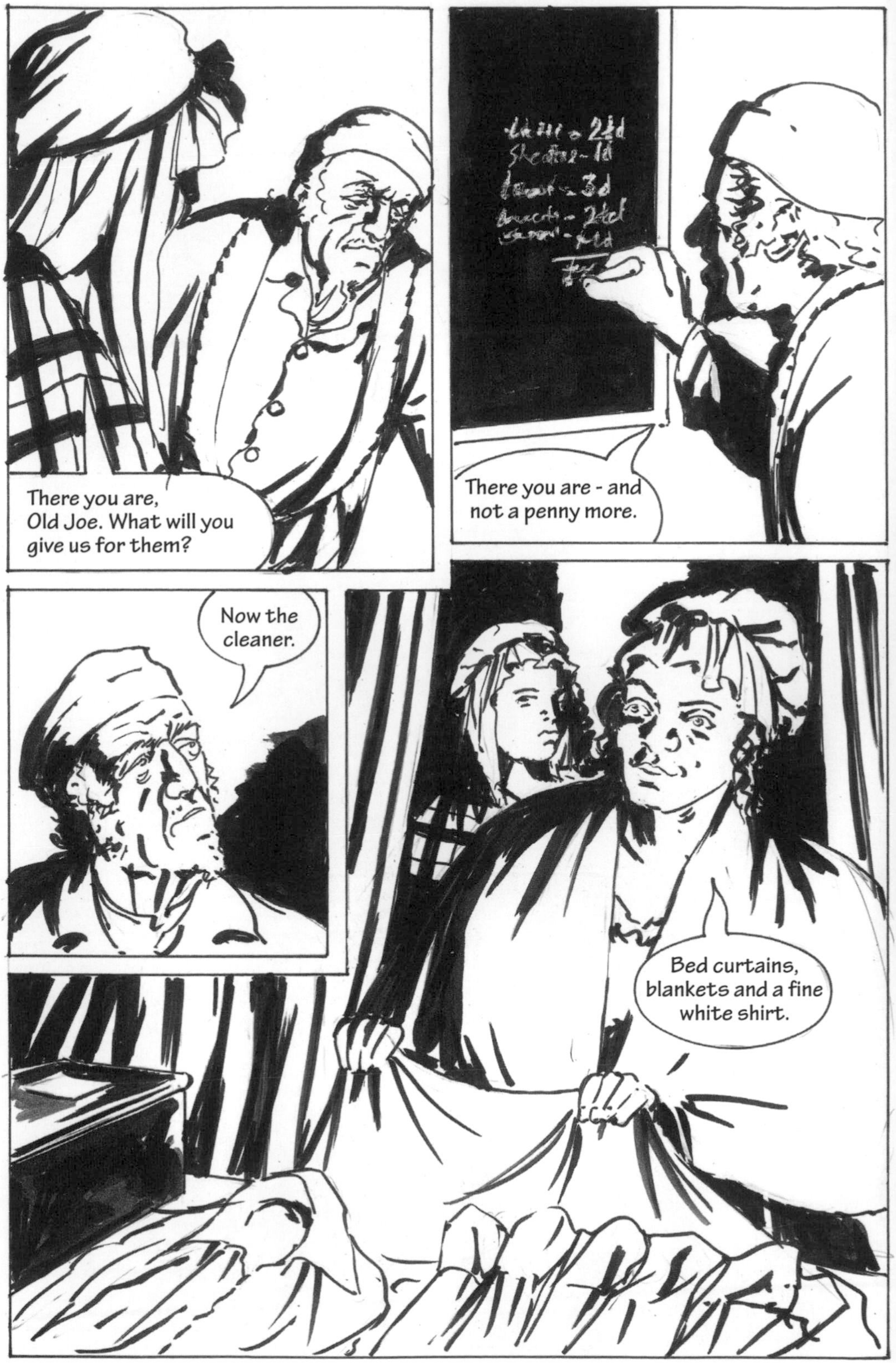
There you are, Old Joe. What will you give us for them?
There you are - and not a penny more.
Now the cleaner.
Bed curtains, blankets and a fine white shirt.

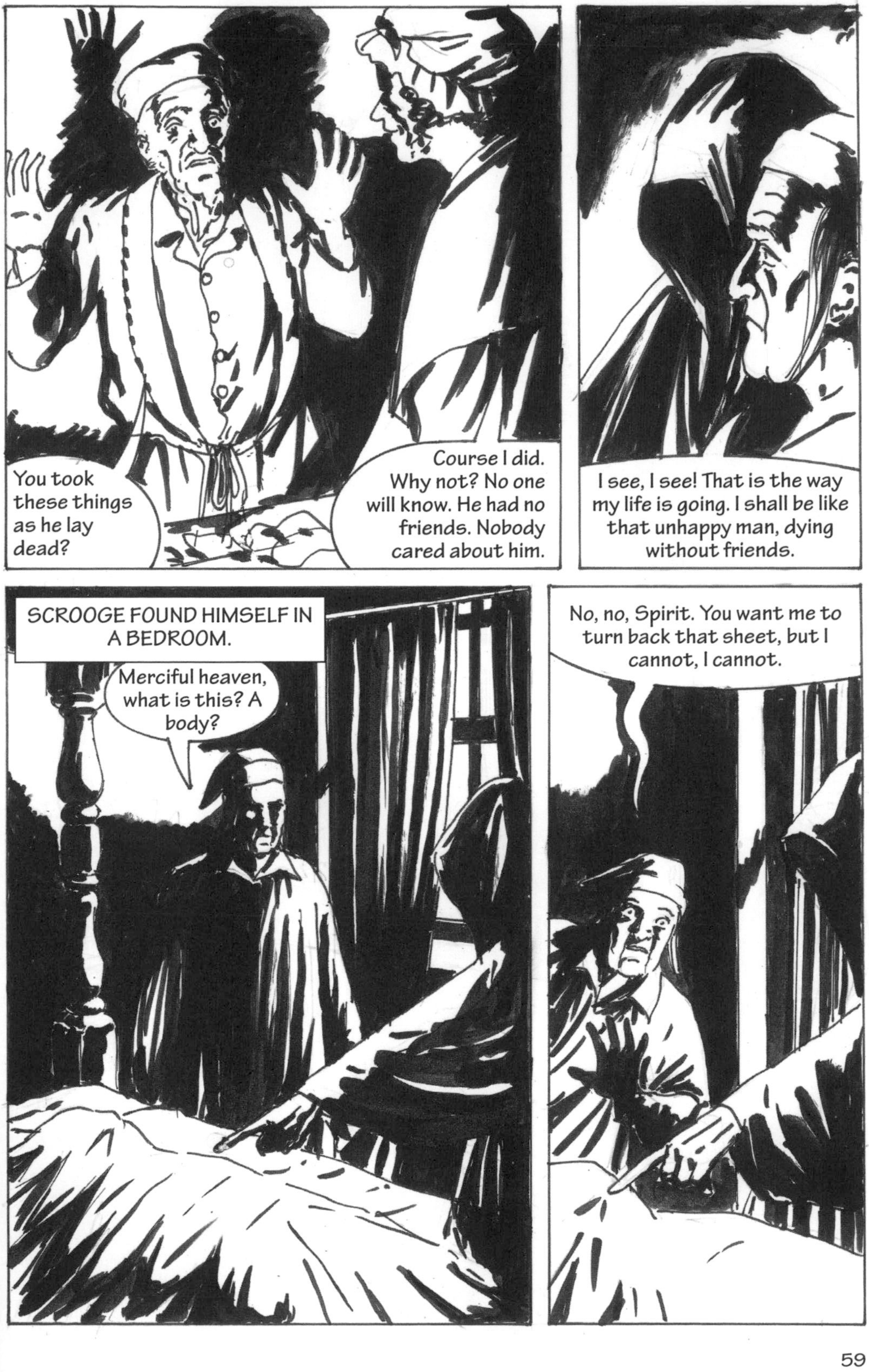
You took these things as he lay dead?
Course I did. Why not? No one will know. He had no friends. Nobody cared about him.
I see, I see! That is the way my life is going. I shall be like that unhappy man, dying without friends.
SCROOGE FOUND HIMSELF IN A BEDROOM.
Merciful heaven, what is this? A body?
No, no, Spirit. You want me to turn back that sheet, but I cannot, I cannot.

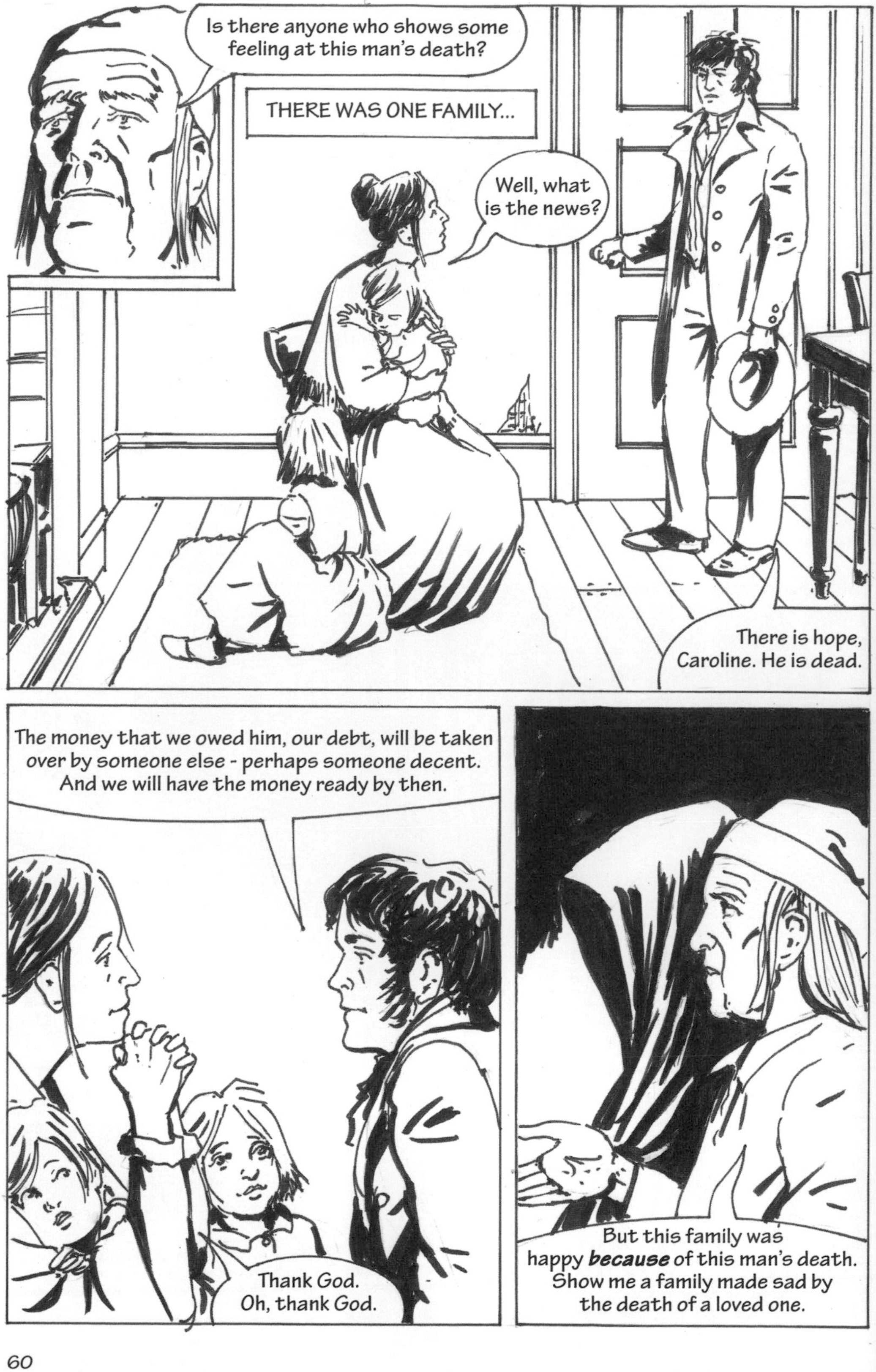
Is there anyone who shows some feeling at this man's death?
THERE WAS ONE FAMILY...
Well, what is the news?
There is hope, Caroline. He is dead.
The money that we owed him, our debt, will be taken over by someone else - perhaps someone decent. And we will have the money ready by then.
Thank God. Oh, thank God.
But this family was happy ***because*** of this man's death. Show me a family made sad by the death of a loved one.

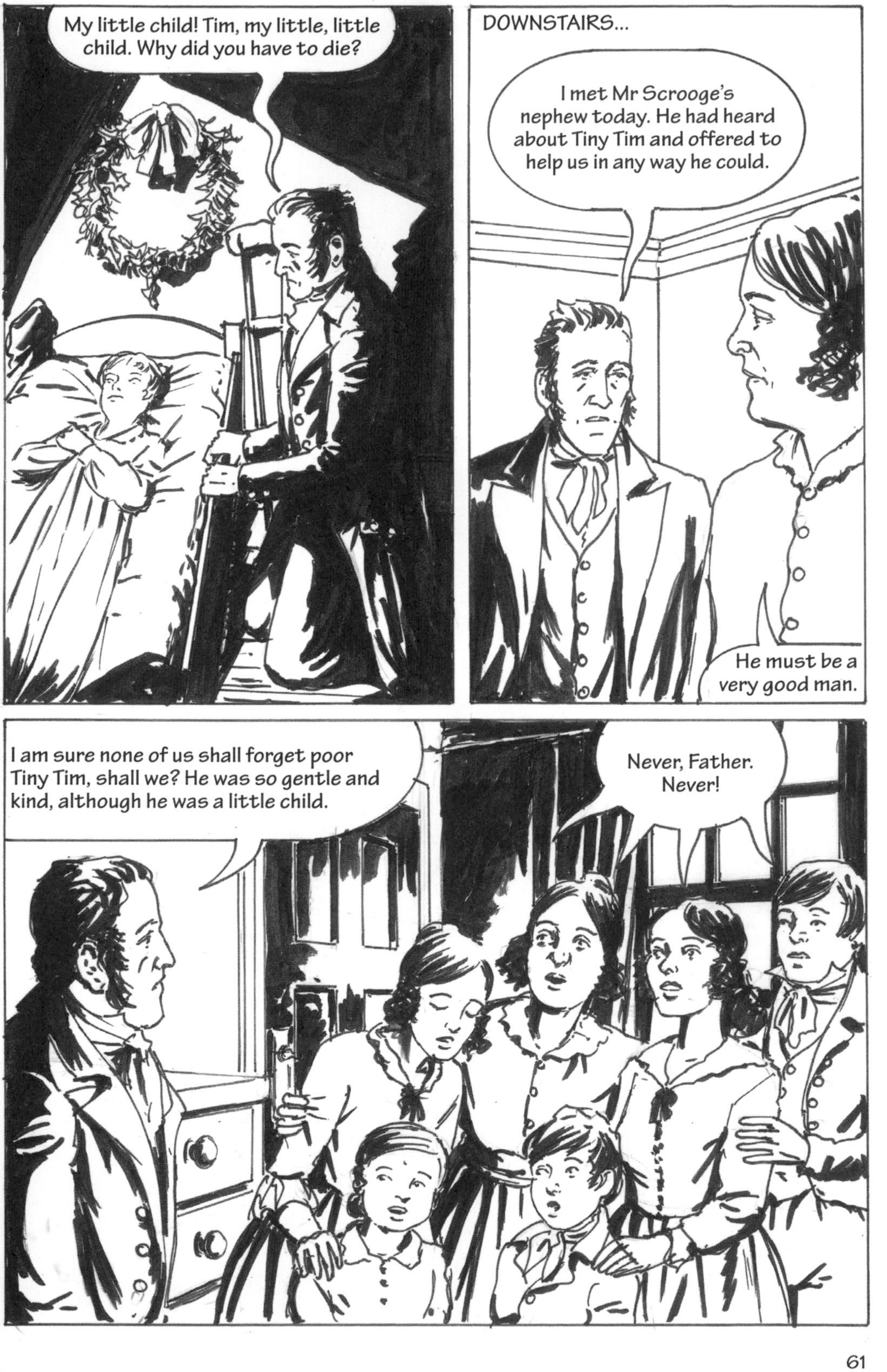
My little child! Tim, my little, little child. Why did you have to die?
DOWNSTAIRS...
I met Mr Scrooge's nephew today. He had heard about Tiny Tim and offered to help us in any way he could.
He must be a very good man.
I am sure none of us shall forget poor Tiny Tim, shall we? He was so gentle and kind, although he was a little child.
Never, Father. Never!

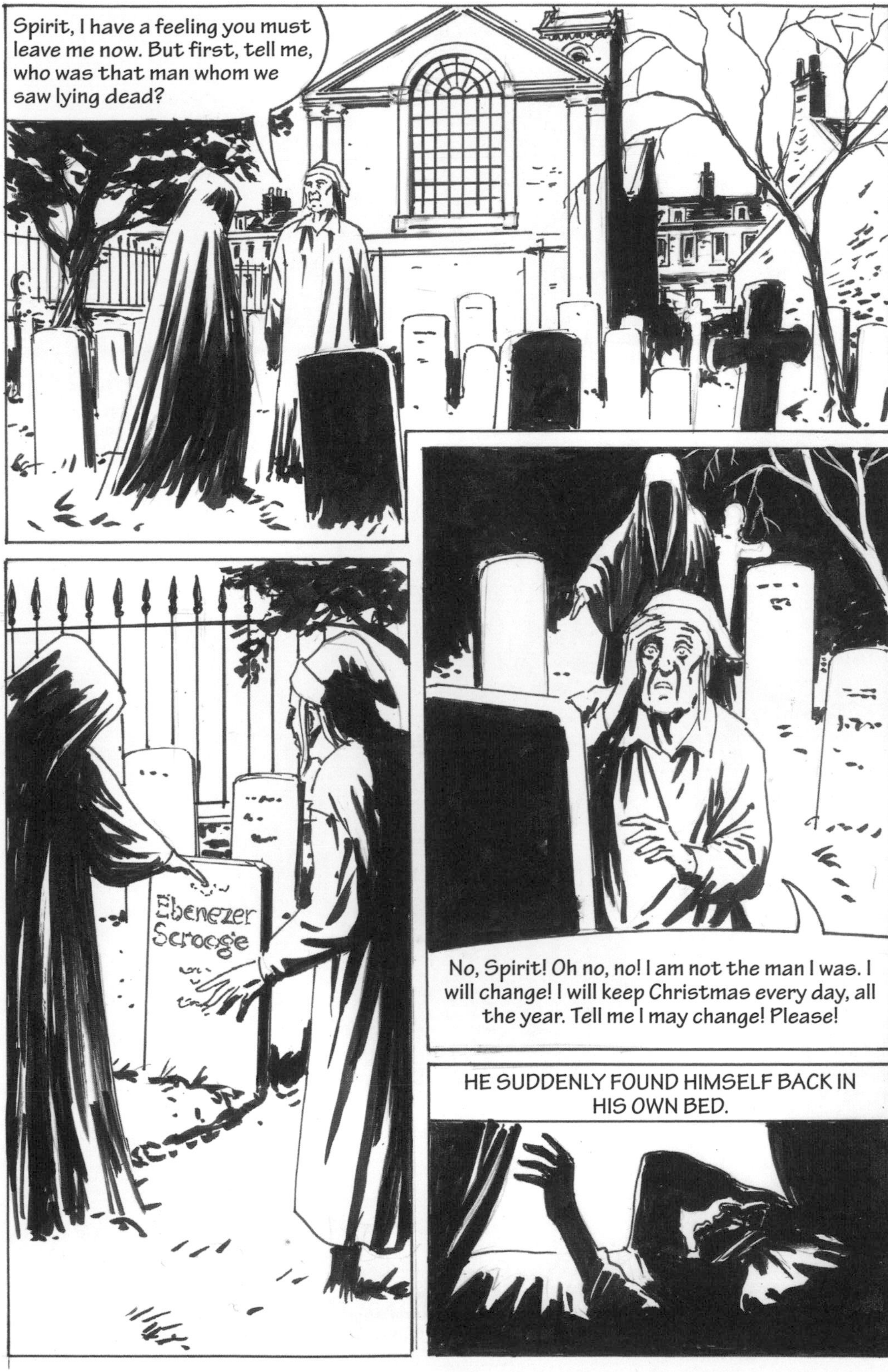
Spirit, I have a feeling you must leave me now. But first, tell me, who was that man whom we saw lying dead?
Ebenezer Scrooge
No, Spirit! Oh no, no! I am not the man I was. I will change! I will keep Christmas every day, all the year. Tell me I may change! Please!
HE SUDDENLY FOUND HIMSELF BACK IN HIS OWN BED.

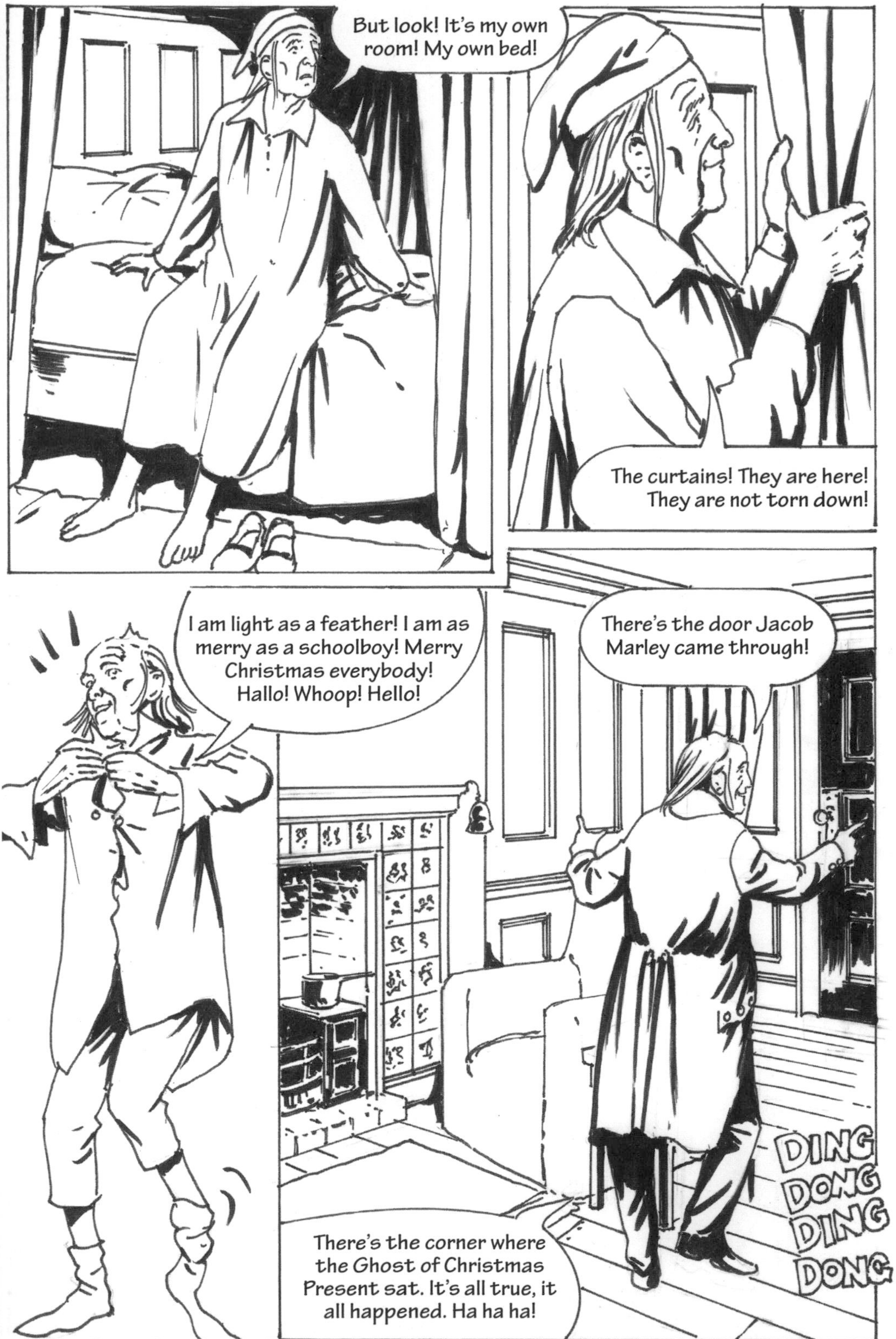

But look! It's my own room! My own bed!
The curtains! They are here! They are not torn down!
I am light as a feather! I am as merry as a schoolboy! Merry Christmas everybody! Hallo! Whoop! Hello!
There's the door Jacob Marley came through!
There's the corner where the Ghost of Christmas Present sat. It's all true, it all happened. Ha ha ha!
DING DONG DING DONG

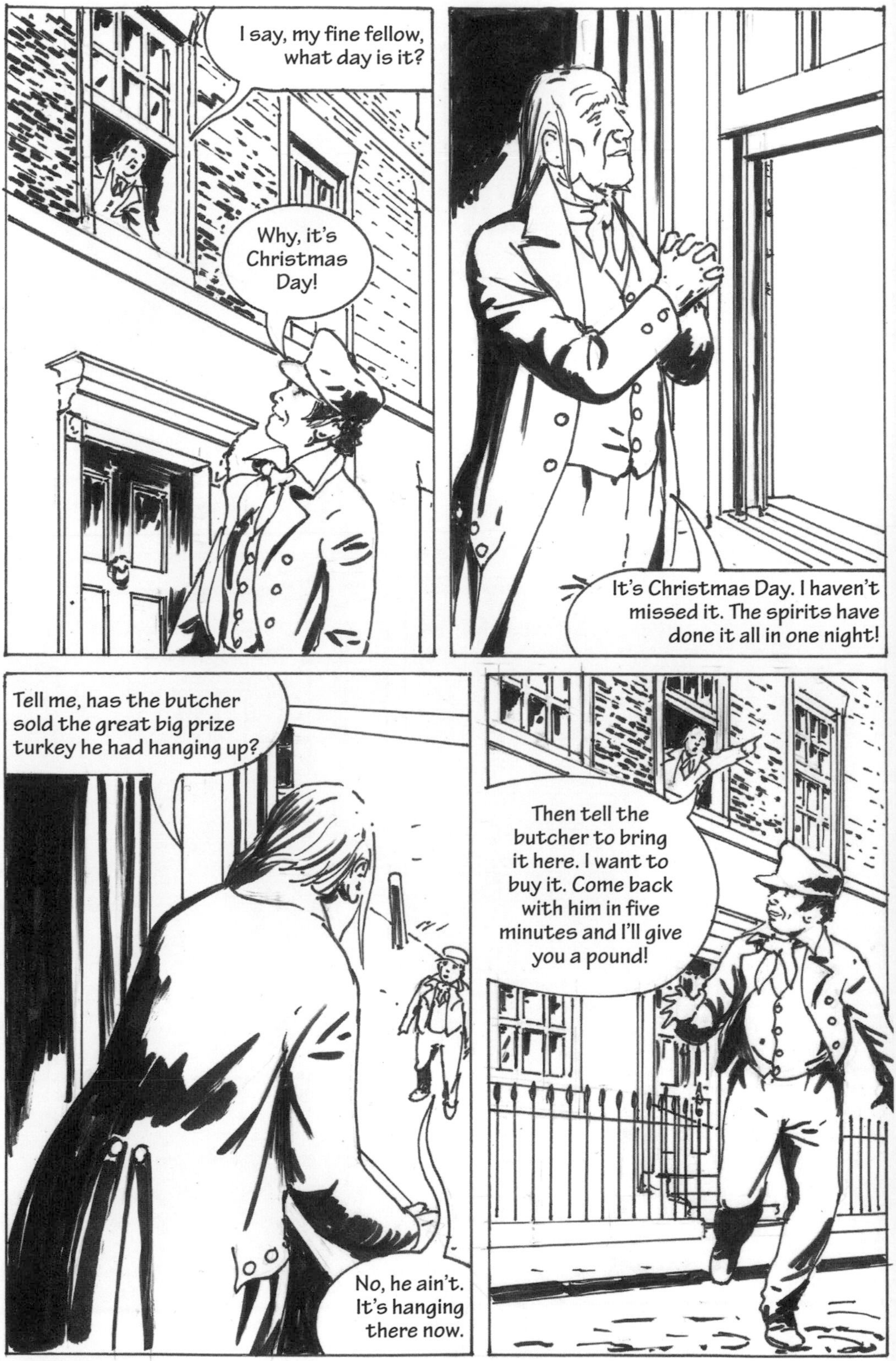
I say, my fine fellow, what day is it?
Why, it's Christmas Day!
It's Christmas Day. I haven't missed it. The spirits have done it all in one night!
Tell me, has the butcher sold the great big prize turkey he had hanging up?
No, he ain't. It's hanging there now.
Then tell the butcher to bring it here. I want to buy it. Come back with him in five minutes and I'll give you a pound!

I'll send it to Bob Cratchit. What a joke. It's twice the size of Tiny Tim!

What a wonderful knocker!

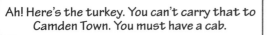

Ah! Here's the turkey. You can't carry that to Camden Town. You must have a cab.

And this is for you, young fellow.

Tee hee - Bob Cratchit will never guess who sent it!

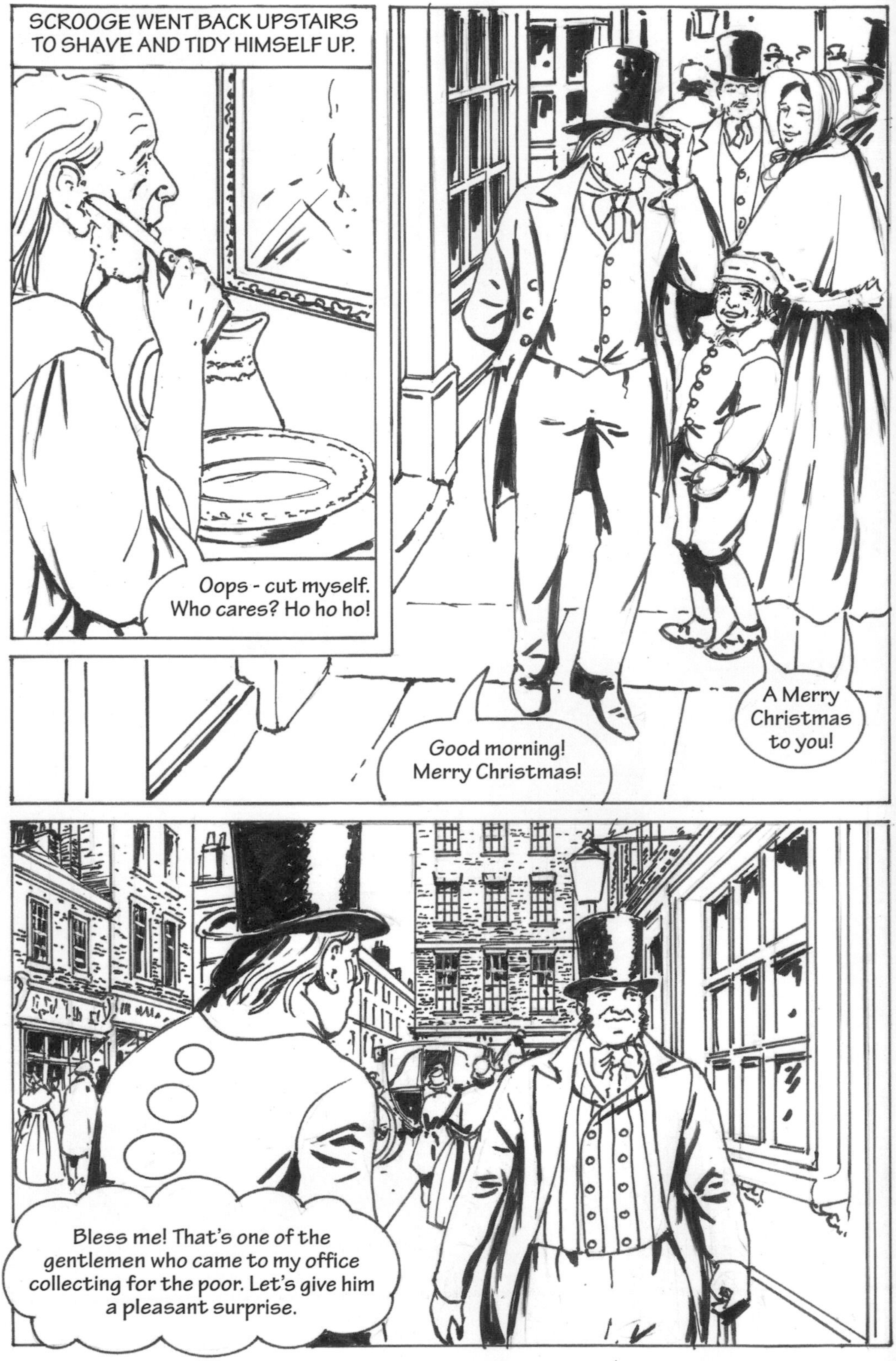
SCROOGE WENT BACK UPSTAIRS TO SHAVE AND TIDY HIMSELF UP.
Oops - cut myself. Who cares? Ho ho ho!
Good morning! Merry Christmas!
A Merry Christmas to you!
Bless me! That's one of the gentlemen who came to my office collecting for the poor. Let's give him a pleasant surprise.

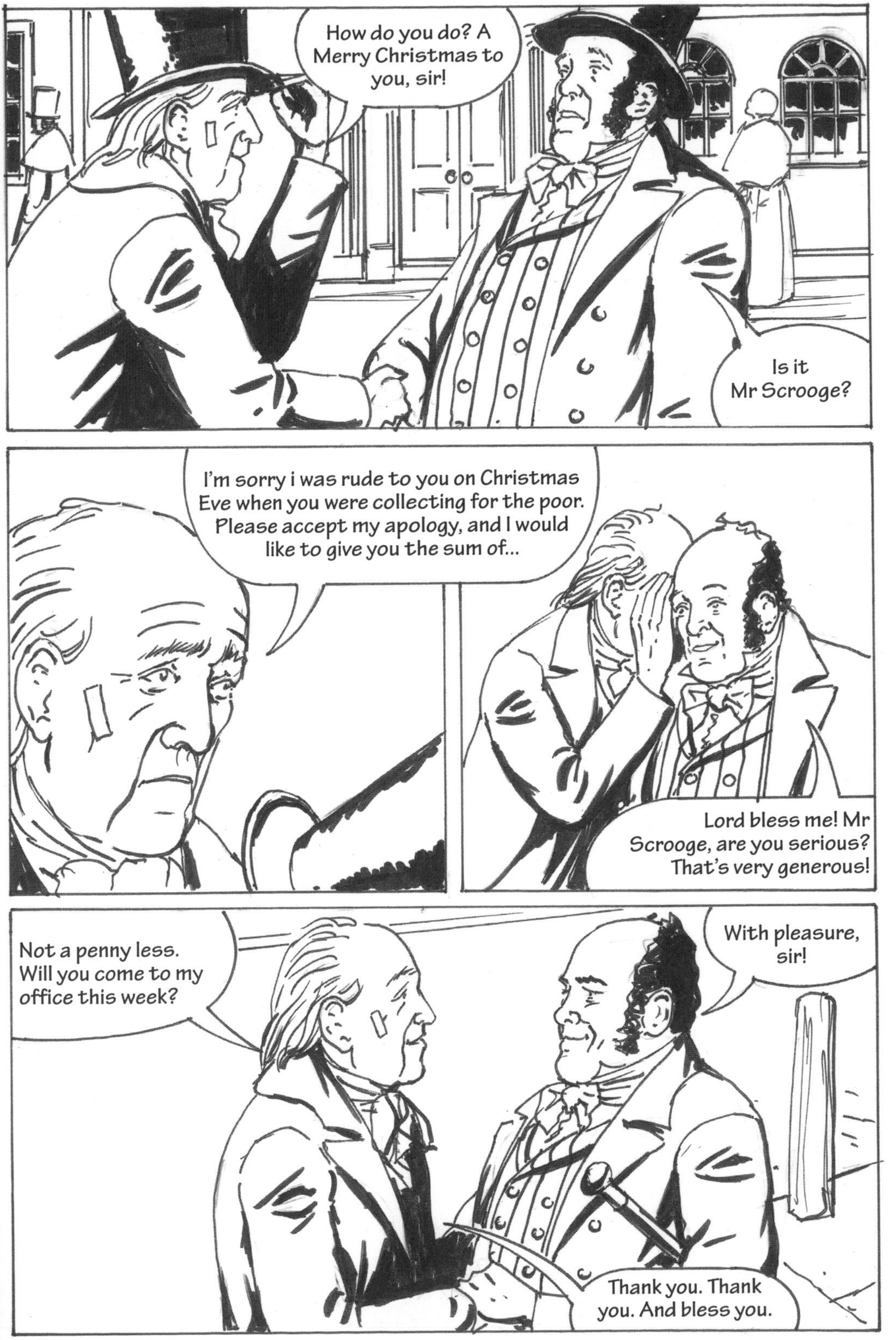
How do you do? A Merry Christmas to you, sir!
Is it Mr Scrooge?
I'm sorry i was rude to you on Christmas Eve when you were collecting for the poor. Please accept my apology, and I would like to give you the sum of...
Lord bless me! Mr Scrooge, are you serious? That's very generous!
Not a penny less. Will you come to my office this week?
With pleasure, sir!
Thank you. Thank you. And bless you.

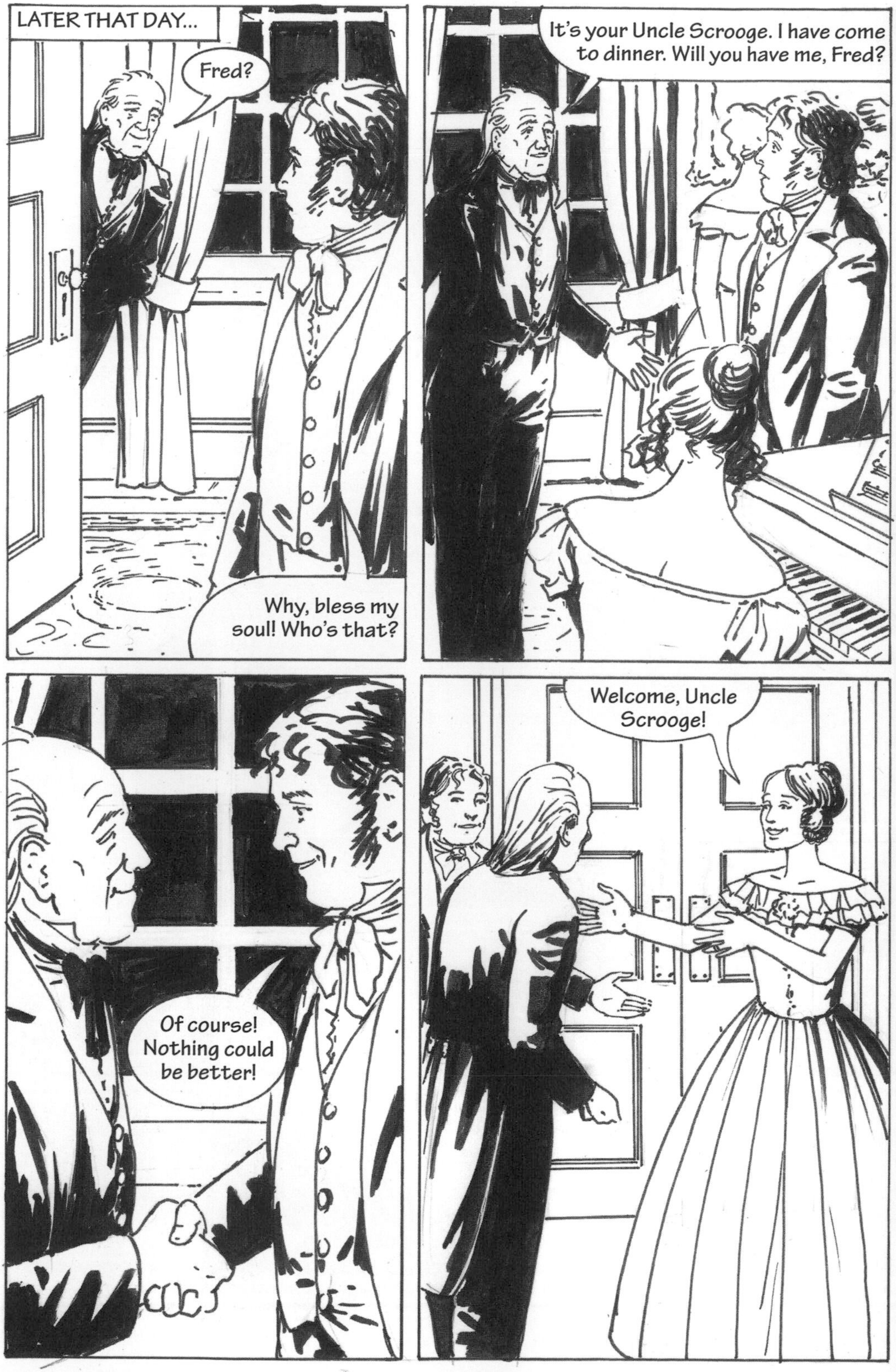
LATER THAT DAY...
Fred?
Why, bless my soul! Who's that?
It's your Uncle Scrooge. I have come to dinner. Will you have me, Fred?
Of course! Nothing could be better!
Welcome, Uncle Scrooge!

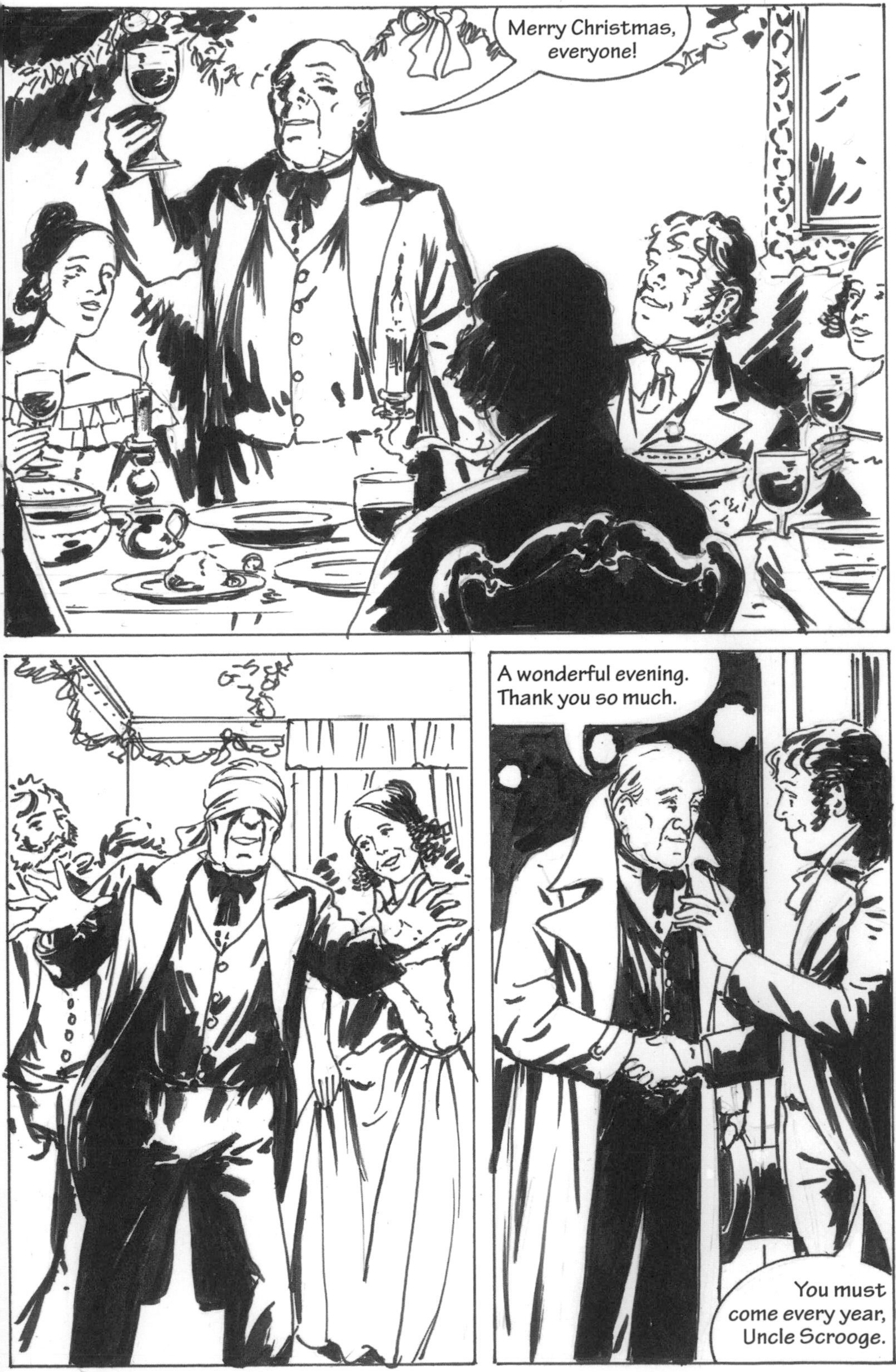
Merry Christmas, everyone!
A wonderful evening. Thank you so much.
You must come every year, Uncle Scrooge.

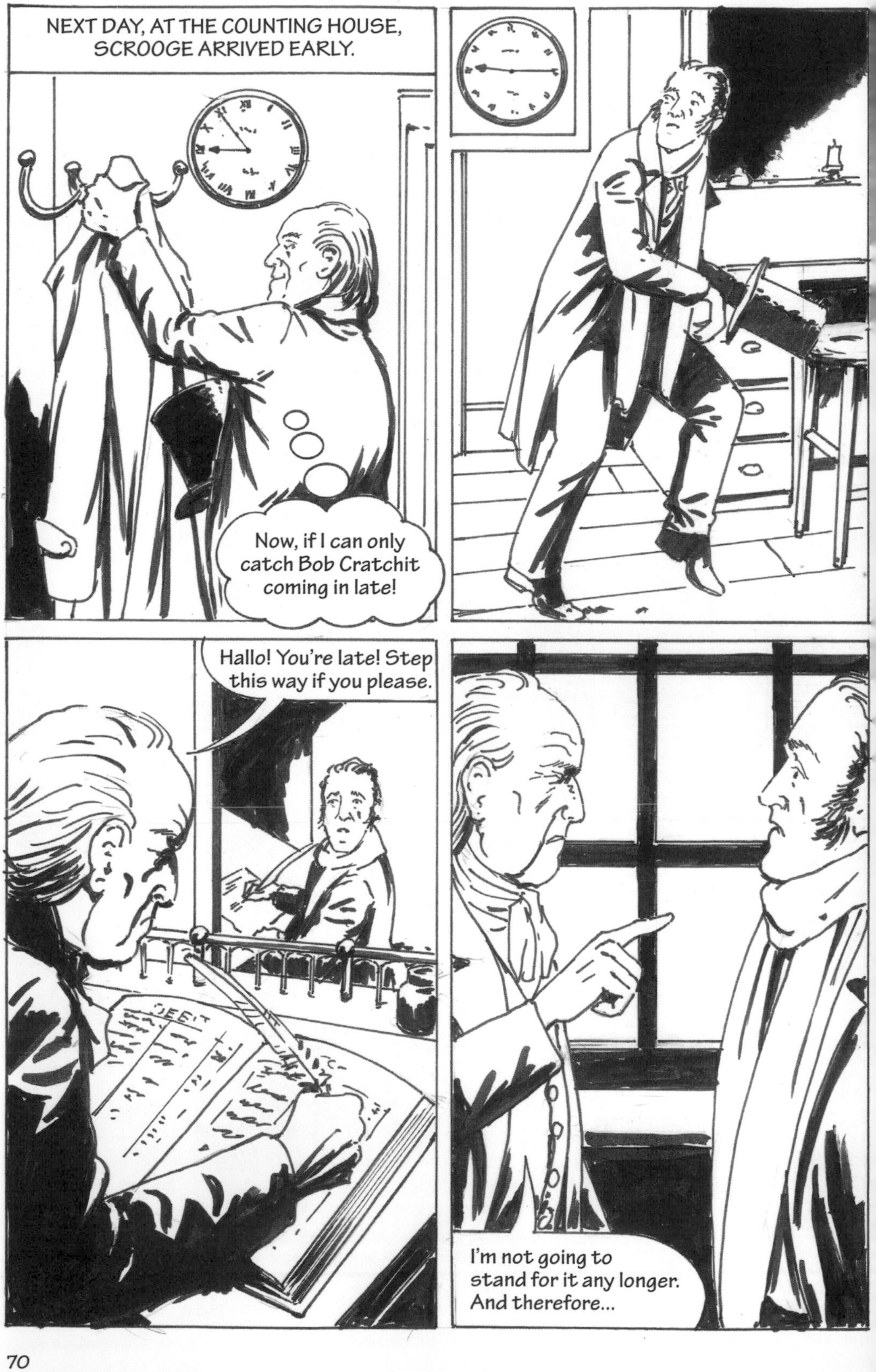
NEXT DAY, AT THE COUNTING HOUSE, SCROOGE ARRIVED EARLY.
Now, if I can only catch Bob Cratchit coming in late!
Hallo! You're late! Step this way if you please.
I'm not going to stand for it any longer. And therefore...

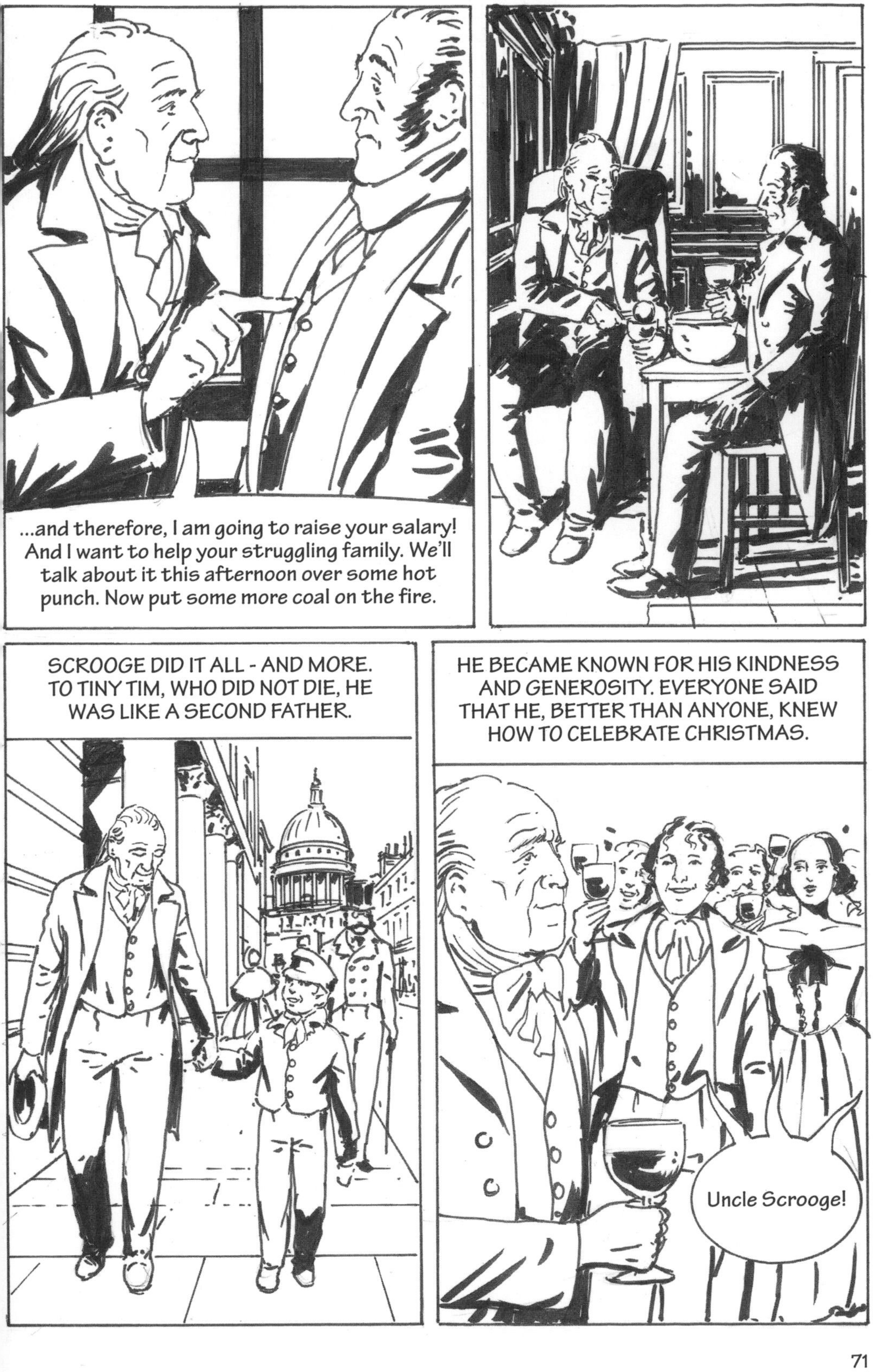
...and therefore, I am going to raise your salary! And I want to help your struggling family. We'll talk about it this afternoon over some hot punch. Now put some more coal on the fire.
SCROOGE DID IT ALL - AND MORE. TO TINY TIM, WHO DID NOT DIE, HE WAS LIKE A SECOND FATHER.
HE BECAME KNOWN FOR HIS KINDNESS AND GENEROSITY. EVERYONE SAID THAT HE, BETTER THAN ANYONE, KNEW HOW TO CELEBRATE CHRISTMAS.
Uncle Scrooge!

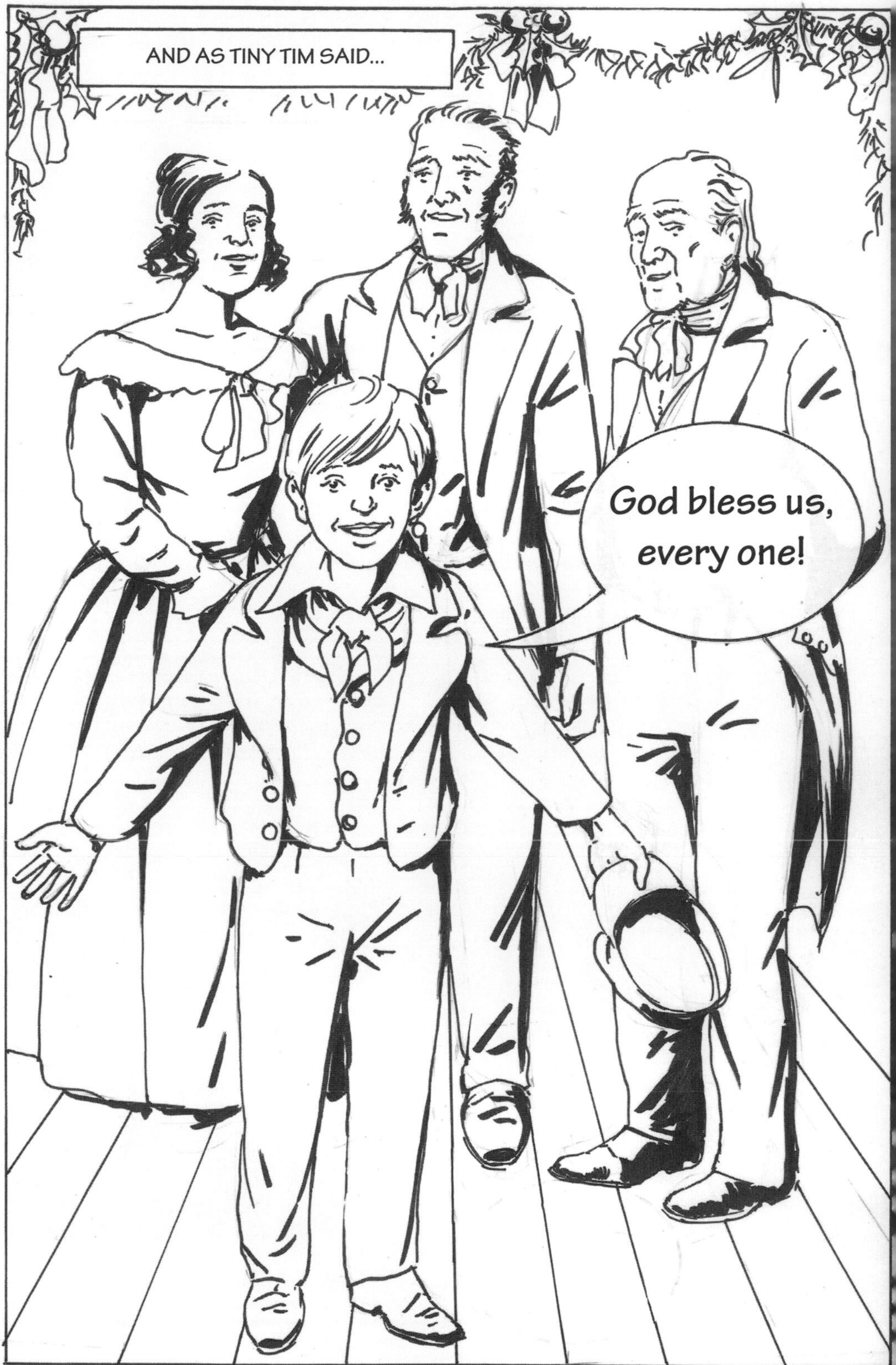
AND AS TINY TIM SAID...
God bless us, every one!